Offside

PLAYING FOR KEEPS DUET

BOOK ONE

SAMANTHA BARRETT

For Leah,
I hope this retelling of your epic could have been fairytale is what
you hoped it would be.
Thank you for the amazing story, covers, graphics and friendship.
This is for you babe xxx

This is your warning!

If domestic violence, bullying, drug use, date rape and degrading is a trigger for you then close the book and move on to another amazing read.
If you are into some dark shit and get off on possessive as fuck asshole alpha males, turn the page babe and wrap your heart in a condom because these boys are about to fuck your feelings, *real hard*!

Playlist

G-Eazy ft Chris Brown – Provide
Chris Brown – Under The Influence (Body Language)
Jennifer Hudson – Spotlight
Bow Wow ft Chris Brown – Ain't Thinkin' Bout You
Jennifer Lopez and Maluma - Marry Me (Kat & Bastian Duet)
Ella Mai ft Chris Brown - Watchamacallit
Ella Mai - Trip

CHAPTER ONE

Darius

I'm back in the halls of CHU. Crestview Heights University is a dreary fun-sucking cesspit of horny teenagers wanting to fuck their way through the cheer squad or the football team. You would think that after leaving high school these idiots would have sorted their lives out but no, all they want to do is pick an easy major so they can breeze through their classes and party all weekend.

"Senior year, motherfucker!" Saint shouts, so Corvin and I head toward where he, Crue and Beckett wait in line at the coffee cart. I shake my head when Saint begins to twerk in the busy line garnering the attention of all the girls nearby. Every guy here hates us but they also would suck a dick to be us for a day. Corvin, Beckett, Saint, Crue and me, we run this fucking school and have done so since we became the first freshmen to ever make the starting team. Girls throw themselves at us, and unlike the others, I don't fuck the same pussy twice. I have a hit and quit it rule as I don't want any of them catching feelings. I don't have time for that shit.

"Smile, asshole, it won't break your face!" I ignore Crue's jibe as I say what's up to Saint and Beckett. Saint has filled out a lot in the off season. The guys and me have been hitting the gym every day and making sure that we stay in shape and don't slack off. I don't want no fucking newbie coming in here thinking they can take our spots! Beckett stands silently next to Saint and Crue, his green eyes scan the area taking everything in. He runs a hand through his Ivy league styled black hair. Beckett is the quiet one out of the five of us. He may not say much but he hears everything. The guy is like a vault and loyal as fuck.

"You coming to Shayla's party?" Corvin asks as he nudges me with his shoulder. I look over at my best friend and give him my best *are you fucked in the head* look. Corvin is a pretty boy, tanned skin, brown hair cut into a pompadour style haircut, light brown eyes and a smile and body that can melt the panties off any girl. We've been best friends since the third grade and are polar opposites. Corvin lives to party whereas I hate crowds and people touching me. "Come on, it will be fun," he tries to plead.

I fight the eye roll that wants to break free. "You said that last time and then you, Saint and Crue rocked up to practice hungover and coach made us all run laps and do drills until you threw up! I am not fucking doing that again." I cut a glare to Saint and Crue when they begin to laugh. Saint is a prankster, always making jokes about everything. He's a fucking player and loves the ladies as much as they love him. With his blond hair, pale green eyes that almost look yellow and the tapper rich boy haircut just adds to the boy next door look he has going on. Crue is the baby of our group. He's a year younger but super smart and skipped a grade in high school. He's got a baby face that all the girls fall for—if it isn't that they melt at the sight of his blue eyes, the fucker is so vain, he spends at least an hour every morning fixing his blond quiff just to make it look the right kind of messy.

"Dude, this is our last weekend before practice starts. Let lose for once. Shit, even Beck is coming and not fighting us." I shoot Beckett a look, he just shrugs and says,

"YOLO and all that shit." Hearing the big fucker say *YOLO* has the four of us laughing and a rare grin making an appearance on his stoic face. Beck is a closed book, Corv and I met him when we were freshmen in high school. He was a transfer and we know he hasn't had an easy life from little things he has said but he never goes into details about his life. When these three hit the parties Beck and I normally kick back at the house. Only the five of us live there and that's how we like it. We never allow anyone into our house or throw parties there, that was my one rule.

"Yeah, alright. I'm in." The three whore's all high-five each other at my agreement. I stand here regretting my decision already. It's not that I hate people, I just don't like them. There's a difference. I hate the fake fuckers who make small talk or the ones who talk too much, I don't even talk to the girls I fuck. I nod, they squeal and follow me to wherever. I *never* kiss them or fuck from the front—doggy style only. The last girl I ever kissed is someone I should never have touched. She was forbidden to me and still I broke the first rule of bro code, *never fuck your best friend's little sister.*

I push through the front door of our two-story ex frat house. The house is fucking dope and it's all thanks to Saint's dad who owns some tech company that he wants Saint to takeover. The front of the house has four large pillars and a little porch with a love seat that swings out front. Inside, it's all hardwood floors, windows and top of the line appliances —our five bedrooms all have their own bathrooms. The basement is set up like an underground club fit with its own bar. We even have a pool in the backyard. When Saint's dad heard we were all going to CHU and found out they were going to tear this old frat house down, he bought and remodeled the whole thing for the five of us. Saint and his dad may not get on and I can't blame Saint for hating the prick, he wants him to give up football and work for his tech company. Saint can't outright refuse or he will be forced to pay back every cent his father has spent on him, he'll get his revenge soon enough.

I dump my bag on the couch and follow the sounds of laughter toward the theater room that is just off the side of the kitchen. I pause in the doorway frowning when the sound of a girl's laughter hits my ears. I grit my teeth, pissed that these fuckers broke another rule, no hoes are allowed anywhere except our rooms. I never bring girls here, nor does Beck. I barge into the room interrupting whatever conversation they were having. My gaze lands on Corvin and I pin him with a look that he knows all too well. He raises his hands in defeat and cuts a glance to the recliner in front of me, I narrow my eyes as I march around to see who the girl is and kick her ass out.

"Oh, he's mad," Crue fake whispers.

"Big mad you mean," Saint joins in, laughing. I don't see Beckett so he mustn't be home.

"Who's mad?" That voice! The moment I come face to face with the owner of said voice my mood sours even further. I stand in front of her, glaring, my nostrils flare at seeing her so relaxed and comfortable in *my* fucking house! The fact that this dirty little liar can sit before me and look annoyed at the sight of me grates on my fucking nerves. The moment her green eyes lock onto mine, my blood begins to boil as memories flash through my mind. Her blonde hair is longer now but I can see some brown tints through it like she has dyed it to look that two-tone color. She darts her tongue out to wet her lips and swallows audibly.

"I thought we said no *hos* in the house?" I grit out, her eyes widening in outrage. I lift my chin in triumph, knowing that my insult hit its mark. Corvin leaps out of his seat pulling my attention to him, his face a mask of anger.

"That's my fucking sister you're calling a whore, asshole.

She can go anywhere she fucking likes in this house, the rules don't apply to her," he snaps. I turn back to face the two-faced bitch who turned my heart to stone as I answer my best friend.

"The rules never applied to her because like the snake she is, she would slither around them anyway." Leah gasps clearly upset at my words. I don't stick around after that, heading straight back out of the house, I jump on my Ducati and peel out of the driveway needing to get the fuck away from her and clear my head. It's all her fault everything went to shit! I have no destination in mind as I fly down the coastal road letting the sea breeze wash over me. Seeing her again has brought all the anger that I fought to keep buried inside me back to the surface. I thought Leah was different. When we were together, she never treated me differently, their family took me in and gave me a home. I gave their daughter my heart and she broke into a million fucking pieces.

It's in this moment a thought hits me, Leah fucked me over so badly I didn't even see it coming. It's my turn for revenge, I'm going to make sure Leah Williams knows just how much I fucking hate her. Her time here at CHU is going to be hell. I'll make sure of it.

CHAPTER TWO

Leah

After Darius stormed out, Corvin, Saint and Crue took me out to a local Mexican restaurant where we sat and laughed for hours before the guys dropped me back at my dorm. Settling into my new school has gone smoother than I thought. I expected to have trouble with my roommate but Cody is actually really freaking cool and loves to hang at the beach like me, is on the dance team I just tried out for and doesn't give a shit what anyone thinks of her! The best part though, Cody doesn't push for answers. When she asked me why I transferred, I clammed up, so she dropped the subject straight away and took me to Starbucks. The week has been a cluster of days with me trying to navigate my way around the new school and finding my place among the hordes of people here.

"What have you got after lunch?" Katie asks from her spot next to me on the picnic table, she is beautiful, legs for days, blue eyes, incredible body and has the blonde poofy *Dolly Parton* hair going on. Oh, did I mention she is from the south and has that crazy, sexy twang to her voice?

"Calculus." I groan, making the girls around me pull sour faces. Cody introduced me to her friends on my first day and we all hit it off. It helps that they are on the dance team and has made getting adjusted easier.

"Girl, you are gonna hate it because Mr. Thompson is an ass," Becca supplies, making me feel even more defeated. I suck at all things numbers unless it's the counts for a routine.

"He fails everyone!" Cody interjects. I peer across the table at her, trying to gauge if she is joking. When she doesn't crack a smile, I drop my head to the table and sigh.

"I'm so fucked," I mumble into the wood, causing the girls to laugh.

"Oh shit, three o'clock. We got incoming!" At the excited tone of Chelsea's voice I perk up and look toward where she said, then scrunch my face. Turning back to the girls, I find them all sitting straighter and pushing their chests out. Well not all the girls, Cody and Katie seem annoyed that we have incoming.

"There's my pretty blonde!" I turn to the side and straddle the bench seat as I look up at my brother and his friends. I learnt on my first day that Corv and the others run this place, they are gods amongst us lowly humans. "Gonna introduce us?" Saint teases as he waggles his brows at me, so I throw him a bone.

"Girls meet the guys, guys meet the girls." Saint narrows his eyes playfully at me before walking around the table and straddling the bench seat behind me and rests his chin on my shoulder. Instead of looking at my brother, my gaze snaps to Darius waiting to see his reaction. It's stoic as usual. Him and Beck never allow you to know more than they want you to.

"Get the fuck away from my sister, asshole!" Corvin snarls as he grips Saint over my shoulder and hauls him away from me by his shirt. The girls, gasp gaining my attention. When I look at them, I find their shocked, almost gleeful gaze on me. I look to Cody for an answer but she just rolls her eyes. Unhelpful much?

"You never told us Corvin was your brother?" Becca says

in the most high-pitched tone, that I'm sure she thinks is sultry and alluring. My face contorts and this is the part that I hate and the reason I chose to go to a different college. Whenever any of the girls find out that Corv and I are siblings they flock to my feet and pretend to be my friend just to use me to get close to my brother.

"Must have slipped my mind," I mutter as I turn back toward my brother and his friends, shooting him a look that I hope conveys *fuck off*.

"Don't look at me like that!" Corv growls. All that earns him is a raised brow from me, prompting him to get to the point of his unwanted visit. "Fine. I came to see if you wanted to come to a party with us tonight?" The moment the words fly from my brother's mouth, I feel *his* gaze on me, burning a path down my body and bringing it to life like no other can.

"I do–"

Before I can finish declining his offer, Becca, Chelsea, Molly and Zara all agree on my behalf. It grates on my nerves but I don't want to cause trouble on my first week here and alienate myself from the friends I've just made, all because they have the hots for my brother and his friends.

"Cool, well come round about eight and we'll leave from ours," Corvin states. I flick my gaze to Darius as I answer my brother.

"I thought no *hoes* were allowed at your house?" Darius's eyes spark with vexation telling me I just poked the bear. I feel the stares of the others on me but my focus is on the tall, dark, handsome man before me. It should scare the hell out of me but it doesn't, all that look does is excite me.

"He didn–" Before Corv can finish speaking, Darius cuts in.

"It seems this hoe is exempt," he snaps before storming off toward the gym. Beckett follows after him without saying a word. Corv sighs and shoots me a sad smile before racing off after his best friend. He has no idea what happened between me and Darius. Corvin just thinks Darius and I hate each other, that wasn't always the case though.

"Don't mind him, babe. He's just pissed because he has blue balls," Crue says as he shoots me a wink, then he and Saint follow after the others calling out that they'll see me later. I can't pull my eyes off Darius until he disappears inside the gym. How can somebody who used to make you feel like the center of their world change in an instant and make you feel like shit beneath their boots?

"Guurrrlll, we need the goss…" I tune out Becca and the others as they all harp on about what they are going to wear and who they plan to suck and fuck. I don't plan on taking them with me. Katie and Cody are more than welcome because unlike the others, they aren't panting like bitches in heat ready to get some meat between their legs.

When will women learn that desperation isn't attractive?

The girls weren't kidding. Mr. Thompson is an ass!

The asshole chewed me out because I wasn't up to *his* level of where he says I should be. He didn't even cut me some slack when Garrett, a friend of Katie's that she introduced me to on my second day, tried to defend me. Instead of him listening to what Garrett and I were trying to tell him he ordered that Garrett be my tutor! Which is why I am now sitting in the library at five p.m. on a Friday night instead of being in my dorm getting ready to hang with my brother and friends.

"I know this must not be how you envisioned your Friday night." I shake my head to clear my thoughts and smile sheepishly at Garrett. He has been nothing but helpful and I would even go as far as to say kind to me, when I have done nothing but be in a sour mood.

"I'm sorry," I say. "I guess I just didn't expect my first Friday night here at CHU to be spent—"

"With me?" Guilt washes over me.

"That's not what I meant." He begins to pack up his books as he speaks.

"It's okay, I get it. You probably have a boyfriend you have a date with and the last thing you want to be doing is staring at my ugly mug." I balk at him, Garrett may be a lot of things but ugly sure as hell isn't one of them. He has this whole football player cross surfer guy look going on. With blond hair with tinges of brown through it, shorter on the sides and long enough on the top for you to run your fingers through, and eyes that are filled with life and laughter. They are an odd color of blue, but with flecks of green throughout them. It doesn't hurt that even through his shirt you can see he has a killer body. Reaching across the table I place my hand on top of his, halting his movements, his gaze cutting to mine immediately.

"I'm sorry if I made you feel that way." Some of the tension in his shoulders eases at my words. "No, I don't have a boyfriend but I do have a brother and I promised him I would hang out with him and his friends tonight." His face lights up and I cringe internally at the hopeful look in his eyes. I may be single but that doesn't mean I am emotionally available. I haven't been available to anyone in a really long time.

"Well in that case, let's save studying for tomorrow?" A smile breaks out on my face as I eagerly nod and start to pack my things away. "We can do this test Mr. Thompson gave you tomorrow as well so then we can chill on Sunday and not have to worry until Tuesday." I beam across the table at him.

"I knew I liked you!" I declare, a tinge of pink hits his cheeks and I have to duck my gaze, not wanting to see the look I know will be in his eyes. I don't want to give him the wrong impression but I also don't want to be presumptuous so I decide to leave things as they are and wave goodbye to him as I make my way back to my dorm to meet Katie and Cody. No sooner do I walk through the door and the girls are on me to hurry my ass up and shower so we can get ready, have some pre-drinks and head over to my brother's place. We may be underage but this is college and who the hell doesn't have a fake ID these days?

After showering and changing into a pair of denim cut offs, I pull on a camo, thin-strapped singlet that is longer in the back and short in the front, short enough to show off the bottom of my toned stomach. Years of dance have been so good to my body and that is the only reason I'm excited for tonight. I can't wait to feel the music and dance to the beat. I slip my feet into my low cut Chucks, dab a bit of lip gloss on my full lips and apply a tiny bit of mascara that I know will make my green eyes pop. I give myself one last once-over in the mirror before deeming myself ready. One thought lingers in my head as I follow the girls out of our room and head for the lifts.

I wonder if Darius will be there?

CHAPTER THREE

Darius

Leaning against the counter, I watch as Leah shows her friends around *my* fucking house like she has the right to! I have to bite my cheek to keep from lashing out at her. Corv lost his shit at me today in the gym. He went on a rant about how I have to let this *grudge* I have against his sister go. Corvin thinks Leah and I stopped being friendly because she told her friends about my mom. That was a lie and the only one I could think of to throw him off track that his sister rocked my fucking world and then blew it apart. Aside from Corv and the guys, Leah was the best thing in my life until she fucking betrayed me!

I didn't give her a reason why I ended things, I just ghosted her.

When Corv and me came back for Thanksgiving one year and she walked through the door with Gary Hayes, my hatred for her only intensified. She knew better than anyone that Gary is and always has been my arch enemy on and off the field. The bastard plays for the dolphins and we are set to play them for the first game of the season. We are the two top teams and they beat us last year in the finals.

"Glare any harder and your face will crack." I turn to see

Beck leaning against the wall opposite me. He has this look whenever he knows something he shouldn't, and right now, he has that fucking look. "How long?"

"How long what?" I snap, He crosses his arms over his large chest and gives me a dry stare.

"How long have you and Corvin's little sister been sleeping together?" I keep my face blank but inside I am a fucking mess. If Corvin ever found out about me and Leah he would kick my ass and I'd let him.

"No idea what you're talking about," I say as I pour myself another drink. I don't like drinking but Leah being around is fucking with my head, so I need something to take the edge off.

"Hm, see, the thing is even when we were in high school you would always pick her out of the crowd. You were always the first to check on her when we got in late to make sure she was sleeping and whenever she needed a ride anywhere you gave it to her." I keep my gaze facing out the window and try to act unaffected by his observations. "Then the last week before we left for college, you changed. You went from being the overbearing big brother to the jealous ex." I spin toward him as that last word exits his mouth. I didn't realize he had moved until we are standing chest to chest. Beck is a few inches taller than us all and he uses that height difference to his advantage.

"You don't know shit," I seethe.

"See, your answer should have been to laugh off my claim or tell me I was seeing things and talking out my ass. You confirmed what I already knew, without *confirming* it." Before I can rip into him, Corvin enters the room. Beck and I take a step back from each other as we face our friend.

Either Corvin is already tipsy and didn't notice the tension in the room, or he just doesn't give a fuck as he saunters over to us, steals the beer from my hand and shouts. "Let's get drunk bitches!"

This is going to be a long fucking night!

🏮

Living where we do everything is within walking distance. Corv, Saint, Crue and the three girls all walk in front of us, while Beck and I take up the rear. Ever since shit with Leah went down, Corv and I have drifted apart. It isn't his fault and he constantly asks what happened to us… why we aren't as close as we used to be. How do I tell my best friend I stopped confiding in him and going to his place for holidays because his sister turned my world upside down?

"I can't wait to dance the night away!" Leah's excitement pulls me from my thoughts. I grit my teeth to keep from lashing out at her and saying something dumb like, *you can dance right the fuck out of my life again.*

"Shayla always throws the best parties," Saint cuts in. "All the cheer squad will be there and those girls can ride a dick like no other." At Saint's words Crue slows his steps until he is walking on my other side, shoves his hands in his pockets and keeps his gaze down. I don't know what the hell is going on with him but I have my suspicions. I just don't want to be the one to voice them until he is ready to admit it.

"Our team could beat the cheer squad," Katie says in a matter-of-fact manner, causing her two friends to cheer and whoop.

"What's the difference between your crew and cheer squad?" Leah balks at Saint like he just said the most insensitive thing in the world. The three girls slam to a stop forcing me to stop walking or risk bumping into Leah. Her back is to me as she stares ahead at her brother and Saint with her hands on her hips. Her perfume assaults me and I fight the urge to not lean in closer and take a whiff—she's always smelt like strawberries and the ocean. A scent I know too well and have grown to hate!

"For one, cheerleaders are there to entertain and hype up the crowd and team through acrobatics, stunts and tumbling. Dancers, our art form is pure, as we tell you a story through the movement of our bodies and make you feel something each and every time we perform." The conviction in her tone as she explains her craft would be awe inspiring if she wasn't such a conniving bitch.

"So, what you're saying, is you can role play?" Saint says as he wiggles his brows suggestively. I shoot him a glare right as Corvin smacks the back of his head.

"You're a real fucking dick!" Corv grits out before continuing on to the party with the rest of us tailing after him. I can feel her peeking over her shoulder at me every few seconds but I ignore it. I've barely spoken two words to her since I left for college. Every time I look at her all I see is her in that bed with *him*! I shake my head to rid myself of those fucking memories, I can't deal with that shit tonight.

Yesterday is history!

I repeat over and over again in my head until we get to Shayla's. The front yard is littered with students drinking from red Solo cups, and at the sight of us, they all come stumbling over to try to gain our attention. The girls flirt while the guys try to appear interesting enough to hold our attention in the hopes of joining our crew, but they will never be one of us. The five of us built something for ourselves that no one can ever take from us—none of our families, except for Saint's, are wealthy, so we built our own wealth and have enough money to live three lifetimes over. I look around the packed lawn and that's when I notice Leah and her friends have slinked off. I dart my gaze around and that's when I spot her on the porch talking to… Garrett-fucking- Jones, her brother's enemy. The guy is vying for Corvin's start position and hasn't been shy about making it known to everyone but *us*.

I'm gonna fucking ruin you, Goldielocks, is my last thought before I sling my arm around some random girl and lead her inside to get me a drink. The moment we pass Leah, I feel her gaze on me, so I turn my head, quirk a condescending brow and shoot her a wicked smirk before pulling the girl under my arm even closer and stalking away from her, relishing in the hurt look in her eyes.

CHAPTER FOUR

Leah

Seeing Chelsea cuddled into Darius's side staring up at him with stars in her eyes and him looking at her like he is mentally undressing her feels like someone poked a red-hot branding iron over my heart. I knew coming here would be hard, but I didn't think after all this time he would still hate me. For months after he ghosted me I had no idea what happened or what I did wrong. When I left for college at BVU, I had no idea *he* would be there. It wasn't a problem at first, we even became friends, until one night, when I was training late at the gym, I heard him and his team talking about my team and who is the most *bangable*. He laughed and told a story about *me* I never fucking knew happened! From that night, everything changed. I was dropped from the team and weeks later I lost my scholarship and had no choice but to transfer.

"You okay?" I pull myself from my spiraling thoughts and focus back on Garrett. I try to plaster on a smile for his sake but I can see I fail miserably when his shoulders slump.

"Yeah, sorry just…yeah," I say.

"Look, Darius and his friends are a pack of jumped-up juice heads who think they are holier than God himself." I can't help it, laughter bubbles out of me at his words because he isn't half wrong. The five of them do prance around with an air of superiority surrounding them. When my laughter dies off, I find Garrett grinning wide at me. He seems more at ease now than he did a moment ago. "Want a drink?" I nod eagerly and allow him to lead me through the hordes of people that are clustered inside the house. Garrett reaches back and grips my hand, pulling me along. I try to spot Katie and Cody but I can't see them among the mass of bodies, Garrett doesn't seem to have any issues finding his way around the place.

As we round the corner and come into the kitchen, my breath hitches at the sight of Darius sitting on the counter with people surrounding him. It's not his popularity that has me short of breath, it's the sight of Chelsea between his legs, running her hands all over him. As if he can sense my gaze on him he shoots me a scathing look that makes me feel like I am discarded trash. Garrett handing me a cup has me tearing my gaze from Darius.

"Do you have anything in a bottle?" He frowns which prompts me to explain further. "A girl can never be too care-ful, ya know?" Realization dawns on him at my words. He leads me to the other side of the kitchen where there are bottles lined up along the counter.

"No sealed bottles but you can pour your own?" I reach for one of the bottles only for it to be snatched from my hand, I snap my gaze over to an angry looking Beckett.

"Beck, what the hell?" I snap angrily. He pulls his heated stare from Garrett to peer down at me. He reaches into the back pocket of his jeans and pulls out a hip flask, making quick work of pouring some into a cup and handing it to me. "Thanks?" I say, slightly confused.

"Next time you need a drink, you find one of us and don't touch any of this shit. Most of it is spiked." My eyes widen in horror as I look from him to the bottles. Beck shakes his head and leans down to whisper in my ear. "Don't trust anyone here, Leah. Word will spread about who you are to Corvin and the wolves will come hunting. You need anything, you come find me." When he pulls back, I stare up at Beckett Dawson in a whole new light. He and I have never been *close* per se but him saving my ass tonight means more than he will ever fucking know!

I'm starting to feel pretty drunk but the atmosphere here is amazing and I feel safe enough to allow myself to let loose a little, knowing my brother and the guys are here keeping an eye on me. Corvin would never allow anyone like *him* to come near me. Knowing that I never have to cross paths with that piece of shit ever again has me feeling lighter than I have in a long time. My mom and dad are so angry at me. They had to take out a second mortgage on the house to pay for me to go to CHU. I hate that they had to do that. I also hate lying to them but I also can't tell them the truth as they would never look at me like I'm their perfect little girl anymore.

"Oh my God! Leah, this is my favorite song. We need to dance!" Katie shouts as she grips my hand and hauls me away from my spot next to Garrett, dragging me over to the makeshift dance floor in the center of the living room. Cody, who was already dancing with some others, squeals at the sight of us and rushes over to give us each a hug. When the beat of *G-Eazy and Chris Brown's* song "*Provide*" flows through me, my body takes on a life of its own as my hips begin to sway side to side. I raise my arms above my head as I let my body roll to the beat. Katie and Cody mimic me for a beat before they let loose and begin dropping down low and slowly working their way back up, pushing their asses out as they go.

The three of us have gathered a crowd, which isn't new to

dancers like us. Guys think just because we can twerk and pop our asses the way we do that we are some horny available women that are begging for their dicks inside us. When a guy I don't know reaches for me, I pull back only to smack into a wall of steel. When my body hums to life, I know who it is without even having to look over my shoulder.

"Shit, sorry, D. I didn't know she was yours." I want to bristle at the way he speaks about me like I am some possession, but the moment Darius's hands land on my waist and I feel him plaster himself against my back, my retort dies on my tongue. His lips brush the shell of my ear and an involuntary shiver races down my spine. Having him this close to me again feels so fucking right. I don't even care if Corvin catches us right now, I want him to know so then nothing has to be a secret anymore!

"Move for me, Goldie." Like a slave to its master, my body obeys. The beat of *Pia Mia's* song *"Do It Again"* pulses and my body moves. I push my ass back against him, and when a hiss escapes his lips, I am filled with a sense of need to have him closer. I reach up and lock my arm around his neck, holding him there while I move against him in time to the beat. Honestly, all I am doing is grinding against his dick but I turn slightly to see a fire burning in the depths of his dark brown eyes. You would swear I'm giving him a competition piece that I have trained months to perfect. His black hair flops forward onto his forehead. I itch to push it back like I have so many times before. He still cuts his hair in that crew-cut style, the five o'clock shadow he now sports only adds to his bad boy vibes. Darius is the epitome of tall, dark and handsome. Unlike other guys here, he doesn't dress to impress. In true Darius Lockhart fashion, he wears his signature white tee, dark wash jeans, shit-kicker boots and his black, yellow and white letterman jacket. "You like that?" I stifle a gasp when he pushes forward and I feel his hard cock poke into me from behind.

"Darius–" I breath out, but he cuts me off smiling and looking at me like he used to. Hope spurs to life inside me at that look—maybe, just maybe he might give me five minutes to talk to him.

"Can you feel how fucking hard I am right now?" I swallow, suddenly so parched and dart my tongue out to moisten my lips and nod. He tsks and shakes his head, scraping that stubble along my cheek again, causing me to shudder. "You know I need the words, Goldie." It takes everything inside me not to moan at the sound of that husky rasp in his voice that I know all too well.

"Yes," I say in a breathy voice.

"Do you want me, baby?"

"Yes." He darts his tongue out and licks my ear lobe before sucking it into his mouth. This time I can't stop the moan from breaking free.

"How badly do you need me, Goldie?" he says before clamping his teeth down lightly on my lobe.

"So fucking bad," I say in a sultry tone I don't even recognize.

"Good." His grip on my waist turns punishing and forces me to stop moving to the beat. "Because you will never know what it feels like for me to fuck you again." I stiffen in his hold as he presses his cock into my ass. "Just knowing how much you want it is gonna make fucking your friend so much sweeter," he snarls before shoving me away from him and pushing his way through the crowd. I'm left standing here, staring at his back until he disappears into the crowd. Shame, guilt, anger and most of all heartache courses through me at his cruel actions and hateful words.

I'm such a fucking fool!

I stand here berating myself as I stare down at my feet until a pair of Air Forces come into view. I slowly raise my gaze to see Garrett standing in front of me with a sad smile on his face. I try to muster a smile for his sake but I can't. Once again Darius Lockhart has proven he has the power to destroy me. Garrett offers me his hand. I stare at it for a beat, unsure what he is asking. He shrugs his shoulders and starts bobbing his head to the beat of Ella Mai's song "Whatchamacallit". When a boyish smile breaks free on his face as he sways off beat I can't help but laugh. He doesn't stop making a fool of himself until I place my hand in his and that is how I spend the rest of the night, dancing with Garrett. He doesn't say anything but I know the only reason he came to dance with me is because he saw what happened with Darius. I decide in this moment, Garrett and I are going to be good friends.

CHAPTER FIVE

Darius

Walking away from her was bitter sweet. She's always known how to move in a way that makes me putty in her hands, but not this time. The moment I saw Corv disappear out the back with Lana, I had to shoot my shot to get under her skin and it fucking worked. I knew she still wanted me, but I needed the proof and last night I got it. Breaking Leah is going to be a lot easier than I thought—seeing her fucking crumble to a million pieces at my feet is going to be fucking amazing.

I wake with a smile on my face as I replay the memories of last night over and over again on repeat in my mind, until I roll over and see my drunken mistake. I wake Carey or is it Chloe? Who the fuck knows and who cares. I chuck her clothes at her to get dressed and usher her from my room as fast as I can. When she speaks and the smell of whatever she drank last night hits me in the face, I fight the urge to gag. The girl looks like a fucking panda with make-up smudged everywhere. I open the door and have to literally push her out it. She spins around with her mouth open to say something, but before her words can make it to my ears I slam the door and rest my forehead against it. I can already tell that girl is going to be a stage five fucking clinger!

"Well that went well." I spin around at the sound for Corv's voice, to find him standing at the base of the stairs with his hair looking like a birds nest, shirtless and in a pair of black sweats.

"Yeah," I say as I head for the kitchen to get some coffee. I'm not hung over but I'm not one hundred percent either. Corvin follows after me and perches his ass on one of the stools at the bench calling for me to make him a cup as well. Silence stretches between us as I wait with my back to him for the coffee machine to do its thing.

"Did you see my sister last night?" I tense at the mention of Leah, and the annoyed tone of his voice has me worried someone told him about me dancing with her. I keep my back to him as I answer.

"Nah, why?" I ask in a bored tone.

"Don't get mad." At the sound of uncertainty in his tone I spin around and pin him with a look that has him throwing his hands in the air. "I said don't get mad!" he pleads.

"I didn't say shit," I defend.

"Your mouth didn't but your face did!" I roll my eyes.

"You fucked Lana, didn't you?" He flinches and gives me an all-teeth guilty smile that has me shaking my head.

"When will you learn?" I say tiredly.

"Dude, the girl can suck better than a hoover and is always down to fuck," he says that like it makes her fucking with his head last year okay. Lana is the captain of the cheer team and a royal bitch. She fucked with Corv's head so bad last year it had him in a dark place. That girl is a fucking basket case and needs to be put into a padded room with the fucking key thrown away.

"No pussy is worth the shit she put you through," I say in a firm tone that I hope conveys my dislike of him going anywhere near that bitch. I turn back to the coffee machine so he doesn't see the look on my face. I know he really cared about Lana and I hate that she fucked him over. When I tried to be there for him last year, he said I couldn't relate because I didn't know what it's like. I wanted to tell him I did but I couldn't without outing myself.

"Enough about her. We aren't getting back together." I snort which he ignores and carries on. "Leah was dancing with fucking Garrett!" That has me spinning back to him. I have to remind myself not to give anything away, so I lean against the counter and clench the granite in a death grip.

"What do you mean?" I push as I try to hold onto my composure.

"Saint and Crue said something happened that upset her and then Garrett showed up and acted like a *gentleman*." He spits the word out like it hurt him to say it. "Then they danced the night away until Beck cut in and walked the girls back to their dorm." I send up a silent thank you to Beckett and remind myself to be on the watch whenever he is around.

"What a dick," I rush to say as I turn back to the coffee maker to fill our cups.

"Yeah. Hey, Leah didn't happen to mention anything to you about why she changed schools, did she?" I hand him his cup of coffee before taking a sip of mine and shaking my head.

"Have you asked your parents?" He sighs and nods.

"Yeah, they just said she lost her scholarship but I know there is more that they aren't telling me, you know?" I nod. His parents are good people. They work hard and have always tried to give their kids everything they need. What they don't know is Corvin is the one who has been paying their bills while stashing the money they think they are paying the bank into a retirement fund he started for them.

"Have you asked Leah?"

"Ask me what?" My gaze snaps to the entryway to see the little devil stroll in like she owns the place. I narrow my eyes when I see what she is wearing—black yoga pants that stick to her body like a second skin, white sneakers and a black sports bra that shows off her perfect tits. Her long blonde hair is piled on top of her head in some messy-looking bun thing, her face is free of make-up. That was one thing I always loved about her, she never wore much make-up because she said if people couldn't accept her the way she was then why should she have to alter her appearance to appear prettier just to make them happy.

"Why you changed schools."

"How did you get in here?" Corvin and I both ask at the same time. When her gaze lands on me, I narrow my eyes. Her green eyes spark with defiance and I know all too well what that look means, she is up to something.

"Corv gave me a key," she says, then saunters over to the coffee pot to make herself a cup. I pin Corvin with a glare.

"Dude, she's my sister!" My upper lip twitches in anger. Rather than be subjected to the torture of being in the same room as her, I dump my cup in the sink before storming out.

"Darius?" Her melodic voice has me stopping in the entryway and tensing when I hear her move toward me. She moves until she stands in front of me, her eyes shining with a cunning look that has me tensing even further. She runs her gaze down my bare torso. When she reaches my shorts, she quirks a brow and smiles. "I hope you don't snore too loud and I promise not to take up too much space in *our* bathroom." My brows jump to my hairline when her words register. I spin around to face a guilty looking Corvin.

"Her dorm block has to be repaired. They have an asbestos problem. It will only be for a few weeks and then you're back to having your own space again," he rushes out, and my nostrils flare in outrage.

"Corv said since you were the only one with a shared bathroom and it is next to the spare room and that it would be fine." The triumphant tone of her voice grates on every fucking nerve in my body. I slowly turn back to face her with a smile on my face that has the one on hers dropping right off.

"I don't snore." Her shoulders relax but I'm not done. "Just FYI though, get some ear plugs because I'd hate to keep you up at night with the screaming coming from my room." Her eyes widen and blaze with anger. I push past her, making my way up to my room. Before I can reach my bedroom, her shout has me grinding my teeth in annoyance.

"Don't call your a hand a girl, Darius, because we all know you *never* fuck the same girl twice!" Fucking little shit! I slam my door closed so hard the pictures on the wall rattle and threaten to tumble to the floor. I pace my room, trying to calm the anger thrumming inside me when an idea hits. Having her next door could work in my favor. A slow smile spreads across my face as a plan formulates in my mind.

Let the games begin, Goldie.

I don't help the others move her shit in as I want them to all know I don't want her here without saying the words. I decide to distract myself by diving into my homework and running over plays for the upcoming season. With our first game being against the Dolphins, coach is going to be riding us hard. We need to win this game to set the bar for the rest of the season. There is nothing worse than losing the first game, it brings the morale of whole team down and once that is gone, it is fucking hard to pick back up.

My vision turns hazy from staring at the plays from last season for hours. I rub my tired eyes and peer over at the clock on my bedside drawer and see it's seven. Fuck, I've been at this all fucking day and well into the night! Pushing back from my desk in the corner of the room, I stroll into the bathroom and turn the shower on. The best part about this bathroom, the mirror never fogs up because both doors on either side always stay open. I strip off and dump my shorts in the hamper in the corner before stepping under the spray, the scalding water burns but it relaxes my taut muscles. I stay under the spray for a few minutes before washing myself and my hair.

Turning the shower off, I grip my towel that hangs over the side of the glass door and wrap it around my waist before stepping out. I shake the water from my hair then run my hand through it to push it out of my face, the moment I do I freeze at the sight in front of me, or should I say the blonde in front of me, leaning against the vanity while shamelessly running her gaze over me. For a split second I forgot about her moving in and being in the adjoining room!

"Take a picture, it will last longer," I growl. Her body may show that she isn't into me but her eyes, they never lie. I see the longing in her green eyes.

"I got plenty of those," she grits out. I step up beside her effectively dismissing her as I grab my toothbrush and start to brush hoping she'll take the hint she isn't wanted here. "You can't ignore me forever, Darius." I rinse my mouth out and take my time about doing it before turning to her and letting my gaze lazily trail over her body. I make sure when I meet her gaze again that all she can see is disgust.

"I don't want to ignore you." Her features soften, I reach out and cup her cheek loving that she pushes into my touch, almost like she needs it. "I want to fucking destroy you and act like you never existed." Her mouth drops open in shock as I yank my hand back and retreat into my room, this time I close and lock the adjoining door.

CHAPTER SIX

Leah

If I thought living with five guys was going to be easy, I was fucking wrong!

I've been here for nearly two weeks and my dorm won't be ready for at least another two to three weeks. Saint has a different girl over every night, Corvin is sloppy and doesn't pick up after himself. Crue is forever brooding and hiding out in his room, blaring music whenever Saint gets home. Beck and Darius are actually okay, well beside the fact that Darius hates me and makes it known whenever we cross paths. The bastard has even resorted to childish pranks like switching the sugar for salt, using all the hot water or dumping my stuff in the toilet in our bathroom. He swears it wasn't him but the laughter that follows proves he's guilty.

Which is why I am currently sitting here in the kitchen on a Friday afternoon waiting for him to come back from the gym. They left about twenty minutes ago and I know it won't be long before he comes running through that door heading straight for the bathroom, that he will find locked. As if the thought of him summons him, he crashes through the door with the shouts of the others following him as he races up the stairs toward his room.

3…2…1…

"Leah!" he shouts my name so loud I cringe, and bite down on my bottom lip to tamper my laughter. I hop off my stool and wait at the base of the stairs ignoring the stares of my brother and the other three at the front door as I stare up at a red faced Darius who is clutching his stomach. "Unlock the fucking doors, now!"

I feign shock. "What do you mean? Is something wrong, darling?"

"*Darling*?" I hear Corvin spit but ignore him. Darius's eyes are blazing with anger then within a split second his face contorts and he hunches over in pain.

"You fucking did this!" he accuses me. I place a hand over my heart and shake my head.

"I have no idea what you are talking about boo boo." The sweet sultry tone of my voice grates on his nerves.

"Fuck!" he screams, before dashing down the hall to Corvin's room and slamming the door behind him. I roll my lips over my teeth to keep my smile at bay as I turn to Corv and the others, then smile sweetly before dashing up the stairs to my room.

Leah – 1

Darius – 0

Since I didn't know we were having a prank war until yesterday, his previous points don't count. I skip into my room and fish the keys for the bathroom doors out of my dresser before going about unlocking them. I decide to take a shower now while Darius is…*busy.* At the thought of him shitting himself I crack up, unable to contain my laughter any longer, tears streaming down my cheeks from laughing so hard.

I wrap my wet hair in a towel before stepping out and wrapping another around my body, the mirror is fogged up thanks to this bathroom having no ceiling fan and the doors being shut. I slide the door to my room open and freeze at the sight of Darius sitting on the edge of my bed with an angry look on his face. I bite my lip as I make my way over to my dresser, if I look at him I know I will laugh and that will just piss him off further,

"Clever, Goldie, real fucking clever." I peer over my shoulder at him and bat my lashes.

"No idea what you are talking about, *Halfback.*" At the use of my old nickname for him, he stiffens. We stand here staring at each other for what seems like hours, but in reality is more like mere seconds before he stands and comes toward me. I turn to face him and back up until my back hits the dresser. He crowds my space, the scent of him invades my senses and it takes more control than I want to admit to not close my eyes and bask in his scent. He cages me in, placing his arms on either side of me as he white-knuckles my dresser.

"You know what this means, right?" His voice is barely above a whisper. I shake my head causing him to narrow his eyes. "I need the words, Goldie."

"No?" It comes out more like a question but I can't help it. Whenever he is this close to me, my brain short-circuits and all rational thought flees. He leans down until his lips ghost over mine causing my heart to thump so hard in my chest, I fear he can hear it.

"You just started a fucking war that you will never win!" he spits before exiting my room without a word, leaving me standing here, strung out and needy. I really need to give myself a orgasm tonight or I risk doing something stupid like throwing myself at Darius and begging him to help get me off like only he can.

"Oh my God!" I cringe at the shriek that comes from Cody and the shouted words from Katie. "You fucking put laxatives in Darius Lockhart's protein powder?" I give her a toothy smile and nod. Katie howls with laughter, Cody joins a second later. I knew he would never suspect me of tampering with his shakes so I thought it would be the perfect prank and it was. I heard him all night groaning and rushing to the bathroom, it was fucking glorious.

"Okay, okay. So now what?" I finally caved and told Katie and Cody about me and Darius and swore them to secrecy—they both agreed. I may have only known them for a short time but I trust them. A measure of time has no say on when you can trust someone so I went with my gut, which told me these girls are trustworthy.

"Now, I guess we wait and see if he softens toward me." Cody and Katie have spent the whole day trying to help me figure out what could have gone wrong between Darius and me, but we came up blank.

"Well until then, get ready," Katie says.

"For what?" I ask.

"We're going to a beach party!" Excitement thrums through me at the prospect of swimming in the ocean.

"I didn't bring anything with me," I say. Cody rolls her eyes and leaps off the bed in their makeshift dorm room that they are staying in until ours is fixed. She reaches into her drawer and pulls out a bathing suit for me and chucks it at me. I hold it up and can't keep the shock from my face.

"I'm just full of surprises, right?" Both Katie and I chuckle. I never thought I would ever see Cody wearing a suit like this but hey, YOLO and all that. After we all change into our bathing suits, I slip my cut-offs back on and slide my feet into my flip flops. Katie clambers over and yanks the elastic from my hair saying I need to leave it out because it adds to the *look*. I don't know what that means, but I also don't argue either as I follow them out of the dorm building. The sun beats down on me and I smile wide, what a perfect way to spend a Sunday. Hanging with my girls and going to my favorite place. I love dancing more than anything but I love the beach just as much. Something about the ocean calls to me. When I'm sad or going through something, like Darius breaking my heart, I would escape to the beach and dance in the sand for hours until my body was so exhausted that my mind couldn't focus on anything else except sleep.

The beach is only a short minute walk from campus. On the way the girls and I chat, they ask me questions and I do the same. They are shocked to learn that Corvin and I are only eleven months apart and are the same age for two weeks out of the year. When we hit the sand I take my flip flops off and carry them in my hand. The moment we hit the shoreline, music can be heard and students can be seen on the bank, the water and some even play volleyball! I squeal in excitement, I love playing beach volleyball.

"Let's enjoy this last day today before our training really kicks in next week." Both Cody and I agree, Katie is right. Come next week, we will be training hard for nationals. CHU has one of the best hip hop programs and has won the state championship two years in a row, our coach, Mrs. Telford, wants to make it three years in a row and has threatened to cut anyone who slacks off from the team. When we reach the party, some of the girls I know from the team greet us but when Chelsea saunters over I can't help the anger that sparks inside me at the sight of her. As she reaches us, her smile appears so fake when she looks at me and before I can call her on it, a shadow falls over me. Turning around and seeing who it is I beam at him before wrapping my arms his waist, hugging him tight.

"Well hello to you to, beautiful." I blush as I pull back. "Ladies," Garrett says to the girls around me. Unlike my brother and his friends, he doesn't preen at the attention the others shoot him, his focus is on me. I know Garrett likes me and I feel bad for him. I've made it clear since we started hanging out that I'm not looking for anything right now. He assured me he understood and hasn't asked me out again since. We still meet up three times a week so he can tutor me. I know he and my brother don't get along but as far as I am concerned that is not my business. "Wanna go play some volleyball?"

"Ye–"

"No, she doesn't." I look to my side to see Corvin and Darius standing there with scowls on their faces. I sigh as I face my brother.

"Corv, we talked about this. Garrett is my friend and you're just going to have to deal," I say with a shrug.

"You fucking him?" My eyes widen at Darius's crass words, while Garrett splutters beside me. Corvin's eye twitches telling me he is pissed Darius asked that but he won't go off at him because he wants to know the answer as well. I look to Darius and my anger soars when I find his glare trained on me. I straighten my shoulders and hold my head high as I say,

"Wouldn't you like to know."

CHAPTER SEVEN

Darius

I grind my teeth so fucking hard I think they may snap when she shimmies out of her shorts and kicks them at my feet before leading Garrett toward the game of volleyball. Corvin is brimming with rage at the sight of his sister in a red, two-piece bathing suit that barely contains her tits, and the bottoms are cut like a G-string and fits into her perfect pert ass with ease. I'll admit, at the sight of her running and seeing her tits and ass bounce, my cock is rock fucking hard in my board shorts.

"Get the guys, we're about to beat this prick at his own game!" Corvin growls. I nod but it takes me a full five seconds before I can peel my eyes off the blonde bombshell who is currently bent over waiting for the other team to serve the ball. Garrett stands behind her with his eyes glued to her ass like he has a fucking right! I head off to find Saint and the others. He's sitting near the keg with his Hawaiian shirt unbuttoned and his abs on display for all the girls to drool over. Crue sits next to him with a sour look on his face, something is up with him and I plan to find out what it is once I've dealt with a certain blonde.

"D-man, what up?" Saint says when I stop in front of him.

I spy Courtney or whatever the fuck her name is out of the corner of my eye, pushing her nonexistent tits out at me.

"Corv wants a game, let's go." At the serious tone of my voice, the smile vanishes from his face and he and Crue are on their feet and shedding their shirts before following after me. I hunt for Beckett on our way to the court but can't find him. The fuckers height would come in handy but no matter, we got this. That's one thing that I love about these guys, we can shoot the shit and fuck around but when one of us needs something, we're all there at the drop of a hat, no questions asked.

"Oh snap," Crue says when we reach the edge of the court where Corv stands with his arms folded over his chest. We step up beside him and I can feel the anger wafting off him in waves as he watches Leah jump around the court. When she spikes the ball over the net and scores a point, Saint has to hold Corv back when Garrett grabs Leah and swings her around. I don't even realize I've moved until a large hand clamps down on my shoulder halting my movements. I look over my shoulder to see it's Beck who stopped me from making an ass of myself. He nods once, asking me if I'm good. I return his gesture and resume my spot next to Corv seething fucking mad.

"Who's sitting out?" Beck asks.

"I'll sit out, Crue is better than me at this shit, plus I'll make sure to cause a distraction." I quirk a questioning brow at Saint, who has a shit-eating grin spread over his face. "Corvin, do you promise not to get mad?" Just then Leah lands another point and Garrett is there to sweep her up into his arms. Corv is clenching his fists so tight that his knuckles turn white. He cuts a glance to Saint as we get ready to hit the court and play Leah's team.

"Do whatever it takes, that fucker isn't winning!" Saint beams and nods like a child who just got his favorite candy. The twinkle in his eye tells me that what he has planned is going to piss me the fuck off. Corvin and I both take the outside hitter positions while Beck takes the setter spot and Crue slips into the spot of blocker. Crue may be the baby of us but the little shit can keep up and he is fucking quick, the competitive streak he has rivals mine.

"Ready?" Nate shouts from the other side as he sets himself to serve. Beck calls back that we're ready. Nate throws the ball and hits it into the air.

"Mine," I shout as I take a step and leap into the air before spiking it down near Leah. She dives for it and misses, letting the ball hit the ground. The guys cheer behind me while I crouch down and meet her angry gaze and smirk. "Losers weepers and all that, Goldie." Her eyes blaze with contempt.

"You haven't won yet, asshole!" she snaps. Our verbal sparring war is over the moment Garrett, the greasy looking fuck ambles over and helps her to her feet. The sight of his hands on her bare hips has me gritting my teeth.

"Set me up. I'm gonna teach that cunt a lesson." I look to the side to see Corvin standing there shooting a death glare at his enemy. I nod and get into position as Beck serves. Corey hits it up for Nate to try a spike but Crue dives for it, hitting it up. I'm under the ball and following Corv's cues as I get close to the net and tap the ball up enough for him. He takes two steps before leaping into the air. I expect him to spike it down and take the easy point but he doesn't, instead he hits it right into Garrett's face. Before his feet can even hit the sand again, he is pissing himself laughing, Crue, Beck and I are powerless to stop our own laughter from slipping free.

"What the hell, Corv?" Leah snaps angrily at her brother. Corv shrugs.

"My bad, your serve. Come on, no time to argue we're burning daylight here!" Corvin sounds like a complete dick but I'm also here for it. "If the pussy can't hack the heat, then get the fuck off the court!" Garrett's eyes blaze with fury but we all know he is too much of a little bitch to ever go head to head with Corv—he'll run away and talk shit about us behind our backs and deny it when we hit him up. The guy is weak as horse piss. Leah shoots me a scathing look which I return with one of my own. When she turns her back to me, my anger spikes as she bends over to help bitch face to his feet. Her perfect perky ass is on display for all to see and I fucking snap.

Marching toward her I duck under the net. Garrett reaches out to grab her hand but I smack it away before he can touch her. She snaps her gaze up to me in shock. I feel Corv and the others at my back which snaps me out of my possessive as fuck mood. What the fuck was I thinking doing this with him here?

"What the hell is your problem?" Leah snaps, placing her hands on her hips.

"You are my problem! Go home and change and stop acting like a fucking hoe!" Gasps sound out around me but it's too late, the words hang in the air between us. I didn't mean to say that but I'm not mad that I did.

"I think the game is over–" I turn my glare at Garrett, who the fuck does this weasel-looking motherfucker think he is butting his nose in to my business? Too far gone to stop myself, I step into him. The shocked look on his face lasts a split second before it's replaced by a smug fake-ass look that I know is for Leah's benefit.

"Stay the fuck out of our shit or you're done here." I may have crossed a line calling his sister a hoe but Corvin tables his anger as he and Beck flank either side of me. Garrett knows we can end him and have him thrown from the school, CHU is nothing without us. We own it. I'm not talking shit either, we actually own the fucking school but no one knows that. We may be gutter rats, well, Beck, me and Crue are. Corv didn't grow up poor but he wasn't rich either. The only one of us who is loaded is Saint. We all made a pact in high school that before we made it out of college we would never struggle again and we kept our fucking word. The five of us are set for life!

"Fuck you, Darius!" Leah seethes as she pushes between me and Garrett. When her back is plastered to his front the cunt smirks sending me into a tailspin. The growl coming from my right tells me Corvin sees what I do, which is why I know I will get away with my next move. I grab her waist and hoist her off her feet. She squeals in surprise but muscle memory is a bitch, so like she has done so many times before, she wraps herself around me. I don't stop moving even when we are off the court and passing her friends, who stare at us like we are a circus act. I feel the guy's eyes on me but I don't stop, not even when I hit the boardwalk, I keep going until I find myself on the road home. "Put me down," she says quietly, neither of us have said a word for the at least ten minutes. I know it's been that long because my house comes into view right at that second.

"Shut the fuck up, Leah." She stiffens in my hold. I don't give a shit if she's uncomfortable. Having her this close to me makes me remember that she is a filthy little liar and can't be trusted! When I reach the front door, I shove it open—we don't lock our door unless we all go out of town as no one here would be dumb enough to ever try to rob us. As soon as I kick the door shut I strut into the living room and drop her. She screams as she hits the couch and glares up at me. "You ever pull a stunt like that again–" She pushes to her feet and gets right in my face.

"You'll what, Darius? Ghost me, shun me, act like I don't exist?" She snorts and shakes her head. "You are fucking pathetic," she snarls as she shoves past me. Like fuck is she getting the last word. I chase after her and shove her against the front door, she has just enough time to stop her face from smacking into the wood by placing her hands out in front of her before I'm plastered to her back, using my weight to pin her there. "Get the fuck off me!" she shouts.

"Or what? What are you gonna do, Leah? You can't fucking get away." I expect her to fight back, scream and curse me out but what I don't fucking expect is for her to burst into tears.

"Please, get off me!" she cries. Hearing the fear and anguish in her voice, I leap away from her and stare like a fool as she drops to the ground. She wraps her arms around her legs and buries her face in them as sobs wrack her body. I scrub a hand down my face, frustrated at myself for caring about her reaction when I should be happy that I finally got her to break.

"Fuck!" I snarl as I bend down and lift her into my arms and head for her room. I carry her bride style up the stairs as she wraps her arms around my neck and buries her face into my naked chest. I fight the urge to tighten my hold on her and demand that she tell me what the fuck has freaked her out. It isn't my business and she isn't my problem anymore, I tell myself as I place her on top of her bed and leave. It takes every ounce of strength I have to not hop on the bed next to her and hold her close as I promise to kill whoever or whatever has her so upset.

"What the fuck was that?" I look over my shoulder to see Corv storming down the stairs toward me. If he wants to punch me then he's gonna have to jump in the pool because I'm not going to let him. Beck, Saint and Crue strut toward us. Saint jumps in followed by Crue but Beck drops into one of the loungers. "Answer me!" Luckily I'm wearing sunglasses so he can't see me roll my eyes at his macho-man display.

"What the fuck do you want me to say? You should have said something the moment we got there instead of letting her parade around like that," I say, motioning with my hands. My excuse is weak but Corvin doesn't care.

"You call my sister a fucking hoe again and I'll break your fucking jaw, Darius, best friend or not, she is my little fucking sister!" My nostrils flare at his claim on her. I want to yell that she isn't his to defend but she isn't mine either... not anymore.

"Got it," I grit out. He shoots me one last look before storming back into the house to go in search of her royal *holiness*.

"You know he means it, right?" I lull my head to the side to look at Crue as Saint hops on the other floaty and nods his agreement to what Crue just said.

"Yeah, well maybe if she dressed properly, Garrett wouldn't be sniffing her like she's a bitch in heat." Saint clucks his tongue, warning me to watch myself. Beck sits up and rests his forearms on his thighs as he stares at me with an unreadable look on his face.

"You sort your shit." I cock my head to the side. "I won't let you break us because you're too fucking stubborn to say what you want out loud. Find a way to deal and tell him." My face tightens in anger as I stare at the fucker, daring him to push me because he knows out of everyone here I am the only one who isn't fucking scared to throw down with him.

"You gonna snitch on me, Becky boy?" He slowly pushes to his feet and moves to the edge of the pool looking down at me, his pale eyes burn with unbridled rage.

"Nah, *D-bag*. With how you are handling having her around and acting like a fucking prick whenever she is near, he'll figure it out on his own." I'm seething with fucking anger when he turns to head back inside. The fucker pauses at the steps of the porch and peers over his shoulder pinning me with a smug look. "Better get that rage under control because Garrett will be here to pick her up in two hours." My eyes widen behind my glasses, muscles coiling tight in anticipation at the prospect of seeing that cunt again today. His face won't survive this encounter! "Better jump on that bike and run away now or risk Corvin seeing that look on your face when she leaves with *his* enemy. Last I recall, you didn't have a problem with the back-up QB until a certain blonde arrived."

Motherfucker!

"You fucked baby sis, didn't you?" I snap my gaze to my side. Fuck, I forgot Saint and Crue were here! "You know what, don't answer that because I don't want to know." I grit my teeth and slip off the floaty, letting the water wash over me hoping it will calm me down enough to stomach the sight of her leaving with another guy. When I break the surface I look at Saint, then lift my glasses off my face so he can see the serious look in my eyes.

"You keep your fucking mouth shut." Crue edges himself forward almost like he is ready to fight for Saint if I were to do something.

"You keep your cock out of her and we have a deal." My grip on my glasses is so tight I fear I'll snap them. "She isn't just a random girl, D. She is Corvin's little sister and has always been off-limits to us. I won't let you destroy this family." Saint's words hit me square in the chest. I can't even form a reply to defend myself because he is right. I never should have acted on my feelings for Leah. I knew if we ever got caught that Corv would lose his shit and it would rock the dynamic of the five of us. That is something I would never forgive myself for doing. These four are the only family I have left and I can't lose them. There was a time I would have taken the risk for the girl because I thought she was worth it, until she ripped my fucking heart out of my chest and spat on it!

CHAPTER EIGHT

Leah

I shift into a sitting position and wipe my tears with the backs of my hands at the sound of a knock on my door. I'm sitting here in an oversize sweatshirt and sweats as I showered and changed after Darius left me. I call out to whoever it is to come in. I'm not surprised to see it's my brother. He takes one look at me and all his anger drains away, his face softens as he makes his way over to me and sits on the edge of my bed.

"I'm sorry about D, he can be a real–"

"Dick?" I supply, he chuckles and nods.

"Yeah. He can be, but he means well." I scoff, which just earns me a stiff look from Corvin. "He shouldn't have called you a hoe." I balk at him.

"Out of everything from today that is all you picked up?" His brow furrows.

"Uh, what else was there?" I throw my hands up exasperated at how dense he is being.

"He carried me off the court and home like I am some errant child! Do you know how embarrassing that is?"

"Well, no." I scowl at the idiot. "In his defense he only did it because he views you as a sister." I fight the cringe that wants to break free. "Seeing you with Garrett and how you were… dressed." I pin him with a look daring him to continue down that path, he wisely doesn't. "Look, Garrett is a dick and is only using you to get at me."

I roll my eyes; men are so stupid. "Garrett had no idea I was your sister when we first started hanging out." That revelation seems to shock him. "Not everything is about you, Corv. I know the five of you are the kings of CHU, but that doesn't mean everyone wants to use me to get to you." His features harden.

"If only you knew," he mutters beneath his breath, which piques my intrigue. We sit here silently for a few minutes lost in our own thoughts until he breaks the silence. "Why did you transfer, Leah?" My heart stops.

"I… uh, I got kicked out of the dance program," I lie. He rolls his lips over his teeth, he knows I'm lying and wants to call me on but I know Corvin, he won't do it.

"Yeah… that's what Mom said." I flinch at the mention of my parents. They are struggling now because of me. They wanted to retire and live their best life but now they can't because paying for my tuition is eating all of their savings and I fucking hate myself for that, but they wouldn't let me drop out of school all together.

I spent the rest of the night holed up in my room, I felt bad blowing Garrett off but he said he understood. I got up extra early to leave the house so I didn't risk bumping into any of the guys. I make my way across campus and head toward the coffee cart to grab me, Cody and Katie a latte. With coffees in hand, I head toward their temporary dorm room. I take a deep breath and steel my spine, ready for them to lash out at me for ditching them yesterday. I knock twice and wait a minute before the door swings open and reveals Cody standing there. I expect to see annoyance at the sight of me in her eyes but when she breaks out into a full blown smile it throws me off kilter.

"Girl, get your ass in here and fill us in!" She drags me into the room and places a kiss to my cheek as she steals her coffee and drops into the desk chair in the corner. Katie sits on her bed and motions with her hands like a child for her coffee.

"Gimme, gimme, I need a caffeine hit pronto for this!" I smile and hand her the cup as I sit on the edge of Cody's bed.

"Girl, spill now!" Cody prompts. I fill them in on everything that happened after Darius carried me off the court and all the way home.

"He is so into you." I pin Katie with a look that I hope conveys that she is nuts!

"Darius hates me," I huff out and drop back on the bed dramatically.

"Babe, if that is what hate looks like then I'mma need him and Beckett to hate me." I turn my head and shoot Cody a playful glare, she puts her hands up as if surrendering. "On the real though, Garrett looked pissed when Darius went all caveman on your ass." I rest up on my elbows and look to both my friends. Katie nods her agreement to Cody's statement which pulls a groan from me.

"I told him I wasn't looking for anything or even interested in dating right now." Katie shoots me a smug look.

"You may not be looking but it sure as hell found you, baby cakes." When they both begin to laugh, I drop back against the bed and groan. Fuck my life. The one guy I want more than anything won't give me the time of day. When we were together, Darius treated me like I was his world, He taught me to view myself in a way no one ever had before. He was the first person to believe in me, that I could make it in dance. I'm eighteen and all I have ever wanted was to dance on stage.

"You okay?" I lift my head from my book and peer over at Garrett. We have taken to sitting next to each other in class now. I'll admit, I have been a bit awkward today, with what the girls said earlier playing on my mind. Garrett is a really nice guy but he isn't the guy for me.

"Yeah, just tired," I lie.

"Want to meet up after school and grab a coffee?" I furrow my brow confused.

"Aren't you meant to be at training?" He shrugs.

"You're worth blowing it off for." Oh God, there it is. I need to distance myself from him or risk him getting the wrong idea. I'm not the type of girl who leads a guy on.

"I have dance practice after school." His face falls, and I feel like shit when he nods and turns back to face our professor. I try to tell myself that I'm doing the right thing but guilt is a bitch and that is why I tack on. "Raincheck?" He snaps his gaze back to me and beams.

"Yeah, of course, I shouldn't miss our first training anyway." How he can go from sad puppy to happy in a split second stuns me but I don't comment. I wave bye to Garrett as I head across campus to meet with the team, excitement thrumming through me and my body starts to vibrate with the need to move. Dance has always been an escape for me. It helped me deal with the darkest time of my life. I round the science building and smack into a wall—correction, not a wall, just Darius. He glares down his nose at me like I purposely ran into him. Not wanting to ruin my good mood, I try to step around him but he blocks my path.

"What's your rush?" Taking a deep breath I crane my neck back and look at him, I hate that his eyes can still hold me captive, they're like a vortex that can suck you right in.

"I have class," I mumble.

"Hm, going to shake your ass, why am I not surprised?" I

bite down on my tongue and count to three to try to calm myself but it doesn't work.

"Coming from the guy who loved it when I shook it for him?" I scoff to drive my point home. Darius strikes out so quickly I have no time to prepare. He grips my arms, then spins us until my back is against the building and he is crowding my space.

"*Used* to like it, now all I can picture is the amount of cocks you've had inside your loose cunt." My eyes widen and my jaw unhinges at his crass words. I shove at his chest but he doesn't freaking budge and that causes my ire to grow.

"Leave me the hell alone, Darius!" I snarl.

"Transfer the fuck out of my school and I will. How trash like you got in here, I'll never fucking know. Open your legs for the dean and he may just put in a good word for you at your new school." I don't know what comes over me but one second my hand is at my side and then in the next, it's cracking across Darius Lockhart's cheek. We both stand here with wide eyes, shocked that I would ever dare lay my hand on him—I've never hit anyone in my life! He bends down until he is right in my face, he is so close his lips ghosts over mine, his brown eyes are so dark they look almost black. "You're gonna pay for that, you washed up has been!" He pushes off me, causing me to smack against the wall harder, turns and storms away, leaving me standing here swarming in my own anger.

Fine, he wants to play this game, then I'll play it better. I'll show him what it's like to play *offside* before I score the final *touchdown*. I decide here and now to put a plan into motion that ensures Darius will be the one stunned the next time we encounter each other. I'm going to make him eat out of the palm of my hand. I just need to keep my heart out of it because it won't survive being broken by him a second time.

I manage to keep up with the team for our first official practice but I would be lying if I said I wasn't beat. My body is aching and my calves are burning from the workout they were put through. I look over at Chelsea and it grates on my frail nerves to see her smiling and standing at attention ready to go another round, the girl is a fucking robot.

"Into positions," Coach Telford shouts. Cody and I groan as we drag our sorry asses over to the others and prepare to run through the routine one final time. Coach told us that the school is considering allowing us to headline the halftime show for the finals of the football game if we make the finals. This would be the first time in CHU history that the cheer squad wouldn't be headlining the event.

CHAPTER NINE

Darius

Coach rode us harder than he ever has before. We're all sweaty fucking messes and my muscles burn in the most delicious way, but I know for the rest of the week I'm going to be fucking sore. We clamber into the locker room breathing like overweight pieces of shit. I ignore the banter of the team and head straight for the ice baths, knowing that is exactly what I need after a training like today. I strip off my clothes and leave them in a heap beside the metal, oval-shaped tub as I climb in. I suck in a sharp breath the moment I hit the water. Gripping the sides, I take deep breaths preparing myself as I slowly slip into the tub. The water is so cold it burns. I slink back and rest my head on the edge of the tub as I settle myself to stay in here for fifteen minutes. Not two minutes after closing my eyes do I hear the guys amble over. I peek one eye open to see Beck, Saint and Crue undressing. Corvin hates ice baths and refuses to willingly get in one. Coach normally has to make his ass and he whines the whole fucking time!

"Dudes, coach is on a warpath," Saint says as he climbs into his bath. Crue hisses like a pussy but not Beck, he gets in the tub on my other side and doesn't need any time to prepare himself, just sliding in like it's a fucking spa bath.

"He has no choice, we have to be ready for the game against the Dolphins in four weeks," Crue supplies. At the mention of the Dolphins, my grip on the edge of the tub tightens.

"They won't win, we got the best QB in the fucking state and Darius is the best halfback out and Beck won't let any of them through. We're solid. That fucker Hayes will be taken down a peg or ten." The guys are the only ones who know what started my hatred for Hayes. I didn't have any reason to hate the cunt, considering he's the QB and not my rival but Corv's. That bastard has had it out for me since we started playing in little leagues and it just grew to the fucking point the cunt fucked my girl at a party. Seeing my arch enemy in the same bed as Leah tore my fucking world apart—that one night changed everything.

"That fucker isn't taking the W, I don't care what we have to do but we are scoring every fucking touchdown!" I growl. The guys nod and grunt their agreement. The bath is no longer cold thanks to the anger thrumming through my veins, if I see her near him at the game I am going to go nuclear on their asses and I don't give a shit if Corvin sees. I'll make sure the whole fucking school knows Leah Williams is a slut and will give it up to anyone.

I kick the stand on my bike down and kill the ignition as I climb off. I peel my helmet off and rest it on the seat as I make my way to the house. I push the door open and freeze at the sound of girlish laughter. I slam the door shut and storm into the living room to find Leah and her two friends Cody and Katie sitting on the couches. At the sound of my arrival they all turn to face me. The two girls look scared—good, they should be. Not Leah though, the dirty little minx sits there with an angry look on her face.

"No hoes in the fucking house," I snarl. Leah's eyes narrow to angry slits.

"They aren't hoes. Believe it or not, not every girl is a hoe, Darius!" she spits.

"Nah they may not be but *you* are!" I snap. Her friend's faces pale while hers slackens with shock. "Have them out of here within an hour... Actually, just fuck off with them. I have company coming over and I would hate for you to finger that used-up cunt at the sounds coming from my room." A hurt look crosses her face but I don't stick around, storming out of the room and heading up the stairs to my room. I kick my door shut once I'm inside and shuck my bag off my back and dump it on the bed before dropping down beside it. I'm full of shit, I didn't have plans for anyone to come over but now, I need to find someone. I pull my phone out of my pocket and scroll through my messages when I spot the unopened ones from Courtney I think her name is. I click on it.

Shit, her name is Chelsea and she is Leah's friend. I don't remember fucking her but I do remember the betrayed look on Goldie's face when she saw me with her at Shayla's party, so I decide she is the perfect person to help me out tonight. I could use a good fuck as I'm too tense and need a release, and it's all the fucking blonde downstairs fault.

> Up to tonight?

I don't have to wait a full minute before her reply comes.
Too fucking easy.

My cock isn't even hard at the thought of her. No girl makes us work for it and that right there is the problem. They think fucking one of us will boost their reputation. It may be but the truth is it just shows how fucking easy they are to give it up to us.

CHELSEA

Coming to yours?

Get here at 8, don't make me wait.

CHELSEA

ohh, I love a man that is demanding. Rawr!

A shudder rolls through me, this girl is going to be another hole I fill for the night and then I'll never think about her again. I look down at my dick and shake my head.

"You better perform tonight and not go soft at the sight of her!" I don't have any fucking trouble getting hard when Leah is around or even thinking about her but the thought of plowing some other pussy has my cock flaccid and uninterested. Not tonight though. I'm going to make Carey scream so fucking loud she won't be able to hide anywhere in this house without hearing her screams.

My phone pings with a message at 7:45.

CHELSEA

I'm here babe X

Babe?

Who the fuck does she think she is? I make my way downstairs and eye Crue and Saint in the kitchen. I pass the living room and see Beck and Leah kicking back watching a movie. At the sound of my footsteps her gaze snaps to me. I shoot her a dark smirk and wink as I head for the front door. I swing the door open and it isn't the sight of her that hits me first it's the stench of the perfume she has drowned herself in. I fight the gag from breaking free and plaster on the most fake seductive smile I can. She stands here wearing a tight one-shoulder crop top and skin tight black bike shorts that hug her like a second skin. Her face is plastered with make-up so thick if you pushed on her face you would leave a dent. Her hair is up in a high pony tail which makes me think she did that on purpose for something to hold onto while I fuck her from the back.

"Hey, sexy," she purrs in what I'm sure she thinks is a sexy tone. I keep the fake smile on my face and step aside for her to walk in. Rather than walk past me she stops in front of me, reaches up on her tiptoes and plants a wet kiss to my cheek. I keep my smile in place and nod, my lack of conversation doesn't seem to deter her. She runs her manicured fingers down my shirt-covered chest and doesn't stop until she reaches the waistband of my shorts.

Only then do I step back.

"Let's take this upstairs." She fakes a shiver, bites her lip. I close the door and turn away to head upstairs but she lurches forward and grips my hand. The only reason I don't yank it free is that Leah is sitting on the couch and staring right at us.

"Oh, hey girl, I didn't know you would be here." Chelsea tries to act surprised but everyone on campus knows who Leah is to Corvin and that her dorm building is being renovated. Leah wipes the look of shock from her face and tries to smile but it doesn't reach her eyes.

"I live here," she deadpans. Enjoying the fact I'm getting under her skin, I pull my hand free and wrap my arm around Chelsea's shoulders and pull her into my side. She molds herself into me, loving this display of ownership she *thinks* she has over me. Leah may not see it but her *friend* views her as a threat.

"Oh ya, kay. Well catch you later." Chelsea flutters her lashes up at me, trying to appear all sexy and shit. It's not working but I play along as I bend down and run my nose along the column of her neck and moan.

"Take that shit upstairs, Leah and I have plans that don't involve an audience who can't fake sexual tension to save their asses." I pull back from Chelsea and snap my gaze to Beckett. Shocked that my best friend would try to rile me up and use the situation between Leah and I against me. I may not have confirmed it, but Beckett knows very well that there is something between Leah and me. He shoots me a condescending look, egging me on to deny his claims and say something but I can't. "Leah *babe*, come sit with me and we'll watch the 365 days movie on Netflix." My grip on Chelsea tightens to the point she lets out a small shriek. I quickly relax myself as I watch Leah stand. She shoots me a look that tells me she is ready to play hard ball even if it means using Beckett to get a reaction from me.

"I'd love to," she says. I harden my features, warning her not to do it but when she looks to the girl tucked into my side and smiles brightly I brace for impact. "Don't fake an orgasm to make him feel better, the poor boy couldn't find a G-spot even if he had a map."

Before I can stop them, words spew from my mouth that never should have.

"Managed to find yours every time!"

CHAPTER TEN

Leah

My eyes are as wide as dinner plates as I stare at Darius, who is mirroring my expression. I tear my gaze from his to see both Saint and Crue standing in the entryway to the kitchen looking between the pair of us. I have no idea what to say or do. Thank God the tension is broken when Beck stands, wraps an arm around my shoulders and speaks.

"Change of plans. Saint, Crue you in for pizza?" Beck asks as he leads me toward the door. I can feel Darius's gaze on me the whole time.

"Hell yeah, we are!" Crue shouts before racing after us. The moment we step out the front door, I'm able to breathe again. As if Beck knows I'm too stunned by that encounter, he doesn't release his hold on me until we reach his car. He opens the passenger door for me and ushers me inside. Working on autopilot, I clip my belt in and wait for him, Saint and Crue to get in. My mind is reeling over what just happened. If Corvin had been home, Darius and I would both be dead!

The guys slide into Beckett's Audi and the tension from earlier returns. In a weird way Darius just outed us to the guys and I have no idea how we are going to keep this *secret* from Corvin.

Beck reverses the car out of the driveway. We're all silent as he drives us away from the house. As the silence stretches my nerves begin to get the better of me but that's not the only thing, my mind keeps wandering back to Darius and Chelsea and what they could be doing right now. I close my eyes and take a deep breath as I try to rid myself of all the nasty images flashing through my mind of the two of them fucking all over the house. My chest aches thinking about him sleeping with her. I never expected him to be celibate or anything but I did expect that the next time we saw each other that he would at least give me a reason as to why he ghosted me for *years*!

"Well this is awkward," Saint mumbles. I cringe knowing that he's right. The ride isn't exactly filled with easy conversation and laughter.

"Yeah, I'm sorry," I say quietly, feeling like shit for dragging the three of them into mine and Darius's...I don't even know what we are doing right now. When my phone rings, I stiffen at the sound of *his* ringtone. I don't even move to pull it out of my pocket, there is no way I am answering that call in the car where the guys will be able to overhear. I'm not a saint but I'm also in a pickle and I don't know how to get out of it without bringing my deepest darkest secret to life.

"You gonna get that?" Crue asks when my phone begins to ring again.

"Uh, no, I'll call Cody back later," I lie, hating that I have to do this to these guys when I've known them most of my life, but I don't have a choice. I don't have the money to pay him, not that he needs it. If I did, I wouldn't be in this position right now! Crue's phone rings and I'm so grateful for the interruption.

"Yo," he answers. "We're just getting some grub then we'll be back so an hour or so tops." He pauses for a beat listening to whoever is on the other end of the call. "Sweet, see you soon." He ends the call and then says, "Corv says we need to have a meeting about… work." His cryptic words have me turning to peer over the seat at him and Saint, neither of them will meet my gaze, I slump back in my chair and look to Beck.

"What do you guys do for work?" I hedge.

"We help out at Saint's dad's company," Beck answers. Call me crazy but I feel like he's lying to me.

"Why don't I believe you?" I retort. Beck flicks his gaze to me for a second before turning back to the road.

"You need to ask Corvin," is all he says, then pulls into the carpark of the local pizza shop. It's run by a beautiful Italian couple that must be in their sixties. All the students come here to eat as they make the best pizza in town, that is for damn sure! Beck parks the car and we all clamber out to head in to fill our faces with some yummy pie!

I've been sitting on the porch steps since we got home twenty minutes ago. I'm a coward and don't want to go inside and see Darius with her. I'm not a jealous person but when it comes to Darius Lockhart, I become this possessive woman who would throw hands if some woman thought they could touch my man.

Worst part?

He isn't my man, not anymore. I grab my phone and unlock it, four missed calls and three texts, I ignore the calls as I bring up the messages.

PIECE OF SHIT

You're running out of time!

PIECE OF SHIT

Don't ignore me, you either pay up or I go public with this.

PIECE OF SHIT

Out for a bite to eat are you?

A shiver runs down my spine, he was watching me and I had no fucking idea. Fuck. How the hell did I get myself into this mess? I didn't do anything wrong, but because of the fucking tape I have no choice. He knows he can do this to me and there isn't a fucking thing I can do about it. I should have gone to the police but I didn't out of fear. When a guy like him takes the stand against a middle class girl like me, who the hell would you believe?

"Hey." I snap my gaze up to see Garrett standing there on the sidewalk. I smile wide, thankful to see a friendly face that isn't team Darius. I hop to my feet and rush over to him. He hugs me and sue me, I return the friendly embrace before pulling back and smiling up at him.

"What are you doing here?" I ask.

"I was out for a run." I run my gaze over him and sure enough, he's decked out in runners, loose basketball shorts and a white tank.

"Of course, sorry," I mutter. He bends down so we are eye level and smiles kindly.

"You look like you need to get out of here, want to hang out?" I don't even hesitate to answer.

"Yes!" He beams, then we walk side by side back toward campus, talking about nothing and anything all at the same time, which is nice. Don't get me wrong, Cody and Katie are great but right now they aren't the people I need to be around because they are team *Da-Leah* and right now, I'm not. Garrett heads toward the coffee cart and orders us a couple coffees before telling me to grab a seat at one of the tables. I do as he says and look around the quad. During school it's bustling with students but after hours it's empty and quiet.

"Here you go." I smile my thanks as I grab my coffee from Garrett. He slips around to his side and sits down taking a sip of his coffee. "Why the long face, beautiful?" I deflate and drop my gaze to the tabletop unsure how to answer or even if I should. The need to talk to someone wins over rational thought, knowing I shouldn't be telling him, but he's my friend and the opinions of the guys shouldn't matter.

"Darius and I had a fight. Corvin and I are drifting apart because I keep pulling away from him. My mom and dad won't speak to me." It rushes out of me so fast that I have to take a deep breath. Garrett doesn't look put out by my verbal diarrhea.

"Okay, one thing at a time. Why aren't your parents talking to you?" Now that I've started I can't seem to keep my mouth closed.

"I lied to them. I told them I got kicked out of my last school but the truth is I dropped out and transferred here which caused them to have to put off their retirement so they could pay for me to go here." Saying it out loud makes me feel even worse than I do already. I don't blame them for being angry with me. I wanted to tell my mom the truth so many times but I couldn't bring myself to do it. If they knew, they would go to the police and I can't relive that shit, I just can't!

"Okay, I'm guessing the reason you haven't told them why you dropped out is that it's something that is embarrassing for you?"

"Yeah, something like that," I mumble.

"Okay, next thing on our list. Why are you pulling away from your brother?" I narrow my eyes.

"You don't even like my brother," I point out, and he shrugs.

"No, I don't, but you're my friend and I care about you so therefore, if being close to my enemy is what makes you happy then I'm here to help." His words shouldn't make me happy but they do. Garrett isn't at all what the guys say he is. He's kind, caring and even... sweet.

"Corv still thinks I was kicked out of school. He has no idea about Mom and Dad not talking to me. I hate myself but I have to do something to my brother that I don't want to and it is going to kill him, but I have to and I hate myself because of that." I'm rambling but fuck, it feels good to finally say that out loud.

"Does arguing with Darius have anything to do with not telling him the reason for the change in schools as well?" I shake my head. I'm willing to talk to him about my parents and Corvin but not Darius, that is one thing I can't trust him with. "The way I see it is you need to give your parents time to come around and realize that their little girl isn't willing to share everything with them. Corvin, well the guy is such a guy, so give him a couple weeks and he'll forget about it." I snort at his reference to my brother.

"You don't know Corvin, he fixates on things and can't let anything go until he has solved it." That's when I remember I need to talk to my brother about this *work* thing Crue and the others mentioned. I know they don't have a job after school. I also know that the things they have in their house aren't from Walmart, they are expensive, so how the hell are they affording it?

"How about we talk about something else to get your mind off all that?" I nod eagerly. "Good, tell me about your new dance routine I saw you and the team practicing in the gym." A smile spreads across my face. I love talking about dance, but finding someone who isn't on the team, who finds what you are saying interesting is hard. All they want to see is you shaking your ass but not how you learned to pop your hip or how you can rotate your body at a certain angle. We spend hours sitting here talking about dance, football and classes. Garrett hangs onto every word I say and I love that.

"We should head back, it's getting late." I peek down at my watch and that's when my eyes widen, it's nearly midnight!

"Shit, I lost track of time!" I rush to say as I jump to my feet.

"It's cool. Come on, I'll walk you home." I'll admit, I swoon like a high schooler. I bite my lip and nod. We fall into step and continue our conversation the whole way home. The walk ends too quickly and I find myself wanting to hang out with him again. We come to a stop on the walkway out front of the house. He doesn't walk me to the door and truthfully I don't blame him, it's not like he's welcome here. "Leah?" I peek up at him through my lashes.

"Yeah?"

"Um, do you think maybe I could take you to the movies on Friday?" My stomach sinks.

"Garrett, I—"

"Just as friends," he rushes to say. I stare at him for a minute trying to see if he's sincere and when I don't see any change in his demeanor, I agree. He gives me a toothy grin before leaning down and placing a quick peek to my cheek that has me standing stiff and stunned. "See ya tomorrow," he calls out as he turns and heads back toward where we came from. When he disappears around the corner, I finally snap out of my shock and head into the house. I climb the porch steps with a goofy smile on my face, grip the door handle but before I can push it open I'm shoved to the side, then pinned against the wall of the house with a hand clamped over my mouth. Fear skyrockets through my body until he moves his face in, his nose touching the tip of mine, but it's his eyes, they are filled with disgust and anger that I almost want to shrink away from him.

"You enjoy your little *date*?" he spits the word date like it burns his tongue. I try to push him off me but Darius doesn't budge. He pushes in closer until his front is plastered to mine. My treacherous body pushes into him loving his close prox-imity. His eyes blaze with something other than disgust, lust flares to life to life in his eyes. He yanks his hand away. I drag a full breath before his lips crash against mine. I gasp, and he uses that to his advantage, slipping his tongue inside my mouth. The taste of him has me snapping out of my stupor, and I wrap my arms around his neck, pulling him in closer.

The kiss isn't slow and sensual, it's a fight for power.

Teeth clashing, but there is a hunger to it, like we both have been starved of each other for so long that we need this in order to survive. It's then that I remember why I was sitting on the steps and hanging out with Garrett and my anger peaks. I bite down on his bottom lip so hard that I taste blood. He shoves me back until I smack my head against the wall. I release my hold on his lip, and he takes a step back, giving me the much needed space that I'll need to think clearly after that kiss.

"What the fuck, Goldie?" he snarls, while cupping his lip. I scowl at the asshole.

"You think you can kiss me after you've been doing God only knows what with that skank?" He drops his hand to his side and smirks, it isn't a sexy smirk it's one that promises pain.

"And I thought that the perfect Goldie liked an open relationship." His words have me frowning.

"What?" He closes the space between us but this time he pushes his leg between mine as he places his hands on either side of my head, caging me in. He lifts his leg a fraction higher and a gasp tears from me when he presses it right against my pussy.

"See." He moves his leg rhythmically back and forward as he speaks. "You think I don't know that seeing her with me pisses you off." A moan tumbles from my lips when he presses his leg harder against me, then he shifts slightly and the moment his leg connects with my clit, I moan.

CHAPTER ELEVEN

Darius

Bingo!

I keep moving my leg back and forward, loving how her eyes glaze over. She may *think* she hates me but her body sure as fuck doesn't. She begins to rock her hips trying to chase the high she knows only I can give her. I bend down and lick a trail from the side of her neck to her ear and nibble on her lobe. She moans and reaches out to grip my waist. I hate that her hands on me have a shiver rolling down my spine.

"You want to come, Goldie?" I whisper in her ear before licking it, causing her to moan again.

"Yes," she pants, her thrusts are growing erratic telling me without words that she's close. "Oh God, Darius. I'm so close," she breathes, my mind is in a lust filled haze, and I drop my leg. She opens her mouth to protest but clamps it closed when I push my hand inside her pants. I don't fuck around, pushing her panties to the side and swiping a single finger through her folds, moaning when I feel how fucking drenched she is. I slip a finger inside her tight wet pussy, relishing in the cry that tears from her lips. I wrap my other arm around her waist to hold her up. I feel her clenching my finger. I insert a second one and love the cry that tears from her throat.

"Ride my fingers and fucking come for me, Goldie!" Like the good little girl she is, she comes on command like always.

"Darius!" she screams so fucking loud I fear she'll wake the whole house and the neighbors. I bring her down from her high gently as she slumps forward and rests her head against my chest. At the contact my mind clears. I yank my hand free and jump back. She stumbles forward a step, then shoots me a questioning look. I keep my face blank of all emotions. "What's wrong?"

I lift my head and harden my features as I say. "Just wanted to prove a point that you really are fucking easy and will let anyone in your pants," I snarl before turning and making my way inside. Before I am out of ear shot I hear her quiet words.

"But you're not just anyone." Hearing those five words come from her mouth has a pang hitting me right in the chest. I would have believed those words a few years ago, but not now. I storm up the stairs intending to go straight to my room but pause at the top of the landing when I see Beckett leaning against the wall shooting me a dark look.

"Don't start your shit," I growl as I stalk past him and head for my room. I can't even slam the fucking door because the fucker follows after me. I spin around and pin him with a look that I hope conveys I am not in the fucking mood.

"You hurt her and you ruin us all," he says in a low even tone. I don't know why but him butting his nose into what I do with Leah grates on my fucking nerves!

"Stay the fuck out of this, Beckett!" I growl as I clench my hands into fists at my sides. The big bastard doesn't heed my warning and stalks toward me until we are chest to chest.

"Everything we have, everything we own is tied into the five of us and I won't let you fucking ruin this for me." I detect a hint of fear in his voice and that is the only reason I back down and step back looking at him in a different light. "Corvin will never allow that to happen—"

"Too bad, Beck, because it's already happened." There is no point in lying, he put it all together himself.

"Darius, we have too much to lose this year with the companies merging, and we need to ace these midterms. If Corv finds out about you and his little sister, it is going to derail everything. Find someone else to fuck and torment but not our best friend's little sister." A whoosh of air escapes me, knowing that he is right. We have all worked too fucking hard to get this merger between BCD'S and Sullivan Global. This merger is everything we have worked so fucking hard to achieve—if we get this deal then that means we finally win!

"Okay," I say on an exhale.

"Don't lie to me, D." I meet his stare with a firm look as I say.

"I won't fuck this up. I need this as much you, Crue and Corv." I don't bother mentioning Saint because his dad is loaded and he'll land on his feet either way this deal goes but for the four of us, this deal is our ticket out of here. I didn't have a dad, the useless fucker skipped town as soon as he knocked my mom up. She was weak and went back to jabbing needles in her arm and forgot she had a kid. I didn't know what it was like to go to bed warm and with a full belly until I met Corvin. He and his family took me in, gave me a safe place to rest my head plus, my mom didn't put up a fucking fight when Mrs. Williams asked if I could live with them. The useless bitch packed my bags herself and I haven't seen or heard from her since.

Beck eyes me warily for a second before nodding stiffly. "Stay away from Leah." is all he says before he turns and walks out of my room. Staying away from the she-devil would be a lot fucking easier if she didn't live here!

I manage to avoid Leah for the next three days, in doing so that means I've had to avoid the guys and most importantly, Corvin. I can't stand there and look at him when all I can think about is how making his sister come on my hand is the hottest sexual encounter I've had in years!

I fucking hate it. I hate her and how the sounds that come out of her mouth as she comes has me burning up inside. My cock is rock fucking hard at the thought of her and how her pussy clenched the fuck out of my fingers like she was milking my cock for all it was worth.

"Where the hell have you been?" I spin around at the sound of Corvin's voice. He marches toward me with his helmet under his arm, his boots sounding like high heels as he moves. The locker room is practically empty except for a few guys. I've been staying out later training each night so I wouldn't run into him in the locker room but I guess my luck has run out. He doesn't stop until there is a foot of space between us, his stare burning into me but I give nothing away. "Out!" he shouts, and like good little dogs the remaining guys clear out at the order of one of their kings. Our word is law and no one wants to fuck with us.

When the locker room is finally empty, I step back and lean against the lockers crossing my arms over my chest. Corvin has a look in his eyes that I know all too well, that look means he knows something is up and will do whatever it takes to find out.

"Why the fuck are you avoiding me?" he growls.

"I'm not," I say in an even tone.

"Bullshit!" he shouts. He's my best friend and has been for fucking years, I hate lying to him but I'm also fucking petrified that if he finds out about me and Leah, I'll lose him and I can't have that. "What the hell is going on, D. Something has been up with you and I want to know what it is."

"Nothing is wrong. I just had shit to do!" I snap. I push off the locker and try to pass him but he shoves me back until I slam against the metal. I shove him back only for him to regain his stance quicker than I expected and get right in my face.

"Fucking tell me!" he yells.

"I want Leah out of the house!" I shout back. His eyes widen and his fury is replaced with surprise.

"Your pissy and avoiding me because my sister is living with us?" The confusion can be heard in his voice, I don't blame him for being shocked.

"She... she just needs to move because I don't like living with her."

"Newsflash, asshole, she isn't moving back to the dorms."

Now I get in his face. "The fuck do you mean?" I grit out. The fucker smiles and it's filled with self-satisfaction.

"Until I find out the truth about why the fuck she *dropped* out of her school and came here, I need her close so I can watch her." I pull back and stare at him.

"What do you mean?"

He sighs then drops his helmet on the bench seat behind us, before running a hand through his sweaty hair. "Mom and Dad are giving her the cold shoulder because she won't tell them why she dropped out. They are stressing because they found out that the Flanders from next door are having to sell because the banks upped their repayments and they think theirs will go up. How the fuck do I tell them I paid off their mortgage and everything they think they pay the bank weekly has been going into a savings for them to retire?" My frustration about the Leah situation flees me when Corv drops on the bench seat and cups his face between his hands. I follow his lead and sit next to him, placing my hand on his shoulder in support.

"As soon as this merger goes through none of us have to hide, but right now with the non-disclosure in place, we can't say shit. BCD'S is going to go global. We dominate the stock market and closing this deal with Sullivan Global will grant us the financial freedom we have busted our asses to achieve from the start." From the moment the five of us decided to start BCD'S we have always pushed to go global with the stock market. This merger means we can own the biggest stock company and hotel chains, shit even the resorts, which in turn means we'll have thousands of employees beneath us and never have to worry about finances again.

"I know. It's just keeping all this a secret is fucking hard when I know I can take their stress away." He turns to look over his shoulder at me. "I can't kick her out, D. I need to know what the hell is going on with my sister. My mom said she went home for a few weeks before coming here. She said something wasn't right with Leah and she was really worried about her." A pit forms in my stomach. Leah and her mom have always been close, so for her to not confide in her mom is so out of character.

"What the fuck happened?" He sits up straight and shakes his head.

"I have no fucking idea. Mom said she wouldn't say a word about what happened and apparently she has cut all contact with her friends at DCU." Davidson Crest University is a really good school. CHU is better of course, but DCU does have the best dance team in the country, so for Leah to drop out and move schools means something happened. Now that my interest is piqued, she isn't going anywhere.

"We need to get her to talk to–" He snaps his gaze to me and raises his brows.

"Don't want to kick her out now?" he says with sarcasm thick in his tone earning him a glare from me.

"Shut up, asshole. Like I was saying, we need to get her to talk and tell us what happened." He throws his hands up in the air in frustration.

"That's the thing, she has pulled away from me. It's not like you and her get along, so she won't talk to either of us." I hate that he's right and it fucking grates on my nerves to hear this out loud.

"She'll talk to Beckett." Corv scrunches his face in confusion so I elaborate. "They have become... friendly and I think she will open up to him if Beck pushes her." Corvin shakes his head.

"Nah, dude, she's my sister," he says as he climbs to his feet. I mimic him and get in his face so he has no choice but to listen to me.

"If you want to know why Leah is running away, then Beckett is your best option." He sighs as his shoulders slump forward.

"Except, Crue, Saint and me have that fucking training camp this weekend and we leave tomorrow night." Fuck, I forgot about that! I don't have to attend because coach said I don't need the extra fitness, but those lazy fuckers do. Serves them right for getting lit every weekend. Beck and I spent more time training than the three of them, which means, we get the perks of *not* spending our weekend spewing our guts out.

"Sucks to be you," I tease. He shoves me back, causing me to laugh.

"You're such a dick."

"I know." He rolls his eyes as he brushes past me, heading to his locker.

"I'll talk to Beck and see if he can talk to Leah," he calls out over his shoulder. I nod and tell him he's making a wise choice but in truth, I don't plan to let Beckett anywhere near her. If anyone is going to find out what the fuck happened, it's going to be me!

CHAPTER TWELVE

Leah

"That's it for the day. There will be a pop quiz on Monday, so make sure you study!" Miss Moss shouts as we all scramble to pack our things and get the hell out of the class to start the weekend. This week has dragged on. Cody and I walk out of our English class exhausted. We have been training before and after school, my body is sore and bruised but Coach said we either train twice a day or drop out. On top of training, I meet with Garrett twice a week now to be tutored for calculus, which I still don't fucking understand. All my other classes have been going great and my professors are so chill compared to Mr. Thompson.

"I need an energy drink or a shot." I laugh and shake my head. Cody is addicted to energy drinks. The girl can go through a six pack of Red Bull in a day and still sleep like a baby at night!

"You need to give that stuff up," I say as we exit the building and make our way to the quad to wait for Katie and Garrett. We have dance practice in an hour and Garrett is going away on some football trip with my brother, Crue and Saint, which means, I'm stuck at home with Darius and Beckett.

Beck is great but without my brother around and Beck knowing about Darius and me, I'm worried he'll try something. We haven't seen each other since he gave me the best orgasm I've had in years!

But of course, he had to go and ruin the moment by talking. To have him bring me to such a high after what happened and not freaking out was a huge thing for me, then his words cut me deeper than he will ever know. I wish more than anything I was able to scrub him from my life so I could finally let him go, except you never really get over or let a guy like Darius go. Not wen he's your first love.

"Grab us a spot and I'll get us some coffees instead." I clear my thoughts and nod as I look around for a vacant table. I spot one near one of the old oak trees and beeline for it. I'm four feet away when I'm gripped by the elbow and spun around so fast, I nearly trip until an arm wraps around my waist to steady me. I look up and still in his hold, when a pair of dark brown eyes stare down at me with an intensity only Darius can master.

"We need to talk," he says in a clipped tone, and releases his hold on me then steps back. I didn't feel cold a minute ago but now without his touch I'm chilled to the bone. It's almost like his touch can set me on fire from the inside in the most delicious way. When he clicks his fingers in my face, I realize I must have been standing here just staring at him. I feel a blush creeping its way up my neck to my cheeks. I shouldn't be embarrassed because he's seen me naked, but with him, butterflies still come alive inside me when he walks in the room.

"About what? If you want to yell about what happened the other night, then I'll pass," I say in a clipped tone as I turn and nab the picnic table before someone else does and honestly, to give Darius a hint that I don't want to talk to him. After he left me on the porch, utterly confused and hurt by his blatant hate, I cried myself to sleep that night and the next. I have no idea what I have done to deserve this type of behavior from him. I should be the one that is angry since he fucking ghosted me!

I feel him slide up behind me and tense. He places his hands on either side of me on the table. I shiver when I feel his warm breath caresses the shell of my ear, he's so close that I feel his body heat radiating off of him.

"Thing is, all I can think about is making you come again but this time, on my cock." My eyes snap wide and I gasp. I'm woman enough to admit that his close proximity and the thought of his cock slipping inside me has me clenching my thighs beneath the table. "Your brother's away for the weekend and I think I need to apologize."

I swallow and dart my tongue out to moisten my lips. "Apologize for what?" My voice waivers and even I can hear how breathy I sound.

"For being an ass. You know I'm always good at making it up to you." I try to fight it, I really do, but a shiver works its way down my spine at his filthy promise. "You remember how long it takes me to say sorry, right?" I slam my eyes closed as memories of how Darius *apologizes* runs through my head. They always end with me naked and spent.

"Uh, hey?" I blink my eyes open to see a confused looking Cody standing in front of me holding two coffees. She isn't looking at me though, she stands there glaring at Darius. I caved and told her about what happened between Darius and me yesterday. She threatened to chop off his balls and burn his eyes out with a hot poker.

"Hey," Darius says in a smooth tone. When Cody looks at me, I shoot her a look, pleading with my eyes to not say anything to him.

"Well nice to see you and all that. Come on, Leah, we have practice and need to meet–" Before I can cut in and stop her from mentioning him, the man himself appears at the other end of the table.

"Hey." I feel Darius tense behind me at the sound of Garrett's voice. Rather than pull back or storm off like he normally does, he whispers low enough for only me to hear.

"If I find out that he has touched you, I'll break his fucking throwing hand and he'll never touch another football, got it?" I gulp and nod, unable to speak and embarrassed as all hell that my two friends are standing here while Darius is plastered to my back, and to top it all off, I now have to go to practice with soaked panties! Darius finally takes pity on me and steps back. I sigh in relief when he heads toward the gym, but calls over his shoulder, "See you tonight, Goldie."

After saying an awkward as hell goodbye to Garrett, thanks to Darius's macho man display, Cody and I headed to practice only for it to run an hour longer because Chelsea and Nikki couldn't keep up with the counts. I'm pissed as hell and fucking aching by the time coach tells us we can leave. She said we could have the weekend off to train on our own time, when we all know it's because she has a weekend away planned with her boyfriend. I grab my bag and sling it over my shoulder as I wait for Katie and Cody. Once they gather their things, the three of us head out. We have barely taken two steps outside before Chelsea is calling out for us to wait. We turn back to see her, Nikki and Becca coming at us. The three of us exchange looks of confusion as we wait to see what they want.

"Hey, babes." I scrunch my face and quirk a brow at Chelsea's fake-ass enthusiasm. She has stopped hanging around us ever since her and Darius *hung out*. "So, what are the plans for this weekend?"

"Nothing," Katie says, sounding just as confused as I feel. Nikki and Becca giggle. Do they realize they look like idiots standing there fake laughing?

"Well, we thought we should totes train, so we were thinking we'll come over around nine?" I reel back in shock at the blatant audacity of this girl. If she thinks she is going to use me to get closer to Darius she has another fucking thing coming.

"Yeah, no." Their fake smiles drop like I knew they would. "If the three of you want to score with the *dream* team find another way, because I'm not helping you bone my brother!" I snarl. Chelsea's eyes narrow.

"Who said I was after your brother?" I grind my teeth in anger. "If I recall, Darius blew his hit and quit it rule for *me!*" I have heard from Katie that apparently that is a thing with Darius, he only sleeps with a girl once and never kisses them.

"Did you want a round of applause for being a slut?" Cody snaps in my defense. My heart soars at her for sticking up for me. I never had any real friends at DCU, they were fake as shit, leaving me to spend most of my time alone and with someone I thought was my only friend. How dumb was I?

"You're just jealous that your bestie's brother isn't interested in your plain ass." I snap my gaze to Cody, her eyes are wide, mouth ajar in shock.

Holy fuck!

Cody has a crush on Corvin and I never fucking knew. She cuts her gaze to me, the guilty look in her eyes spears me.

"Leah, I had no idea he was your brother and I've never done anything with him, I swear. I would never do anything with him now because of girl code and you're my girl." Call me stupid, but I believe her. I can't be friends with girls who are going after my brother because it's just icky!

I shrug and smile as I say, "I know you wouldn't." A whoosh of air escapes her. "I have to go, but you and Katie come round tomorrow and we'll practice and swim, it's only Beck–" I turn back to Chelsea as I finish speaking, "and

Darius home." Katie and Cody agree, giving me a hug each as I head home.

I'm just around the corner from the house when my phone rings. At the sound of *his* ringtone, I tense up. I pull my phone out and answer it before I chicken out, knowing I can't keep ignoring him forever.

"What?" I snap.

"Now, now, is that any way to greet me?" I grit my teeth and breath through my nose as I try to calm the fury spurring to life inside me at the sound of his nasally voice.

"What can I do for you?" I say in a sickly-sweet voice.

"You can start by doing what I fucking told you to do! You're running out of time. The game is in three weeks and they won't be taking the field!" Guilt and shame war inside me. If I do what he is asking, I'll ruin them and they will never forgive me! I've tried for weeks to build up the courage to tell Corvin but I can never get the words out.

"Why are you doing this?"

"Because I fucking can! Those five are going to learn a fucking lesson that they aren't untouchable!"

"I... I'll go to the cops and tell them everything," I threaten.

"Go tell them. We all know they won't do shit because of who I am and where I come from. You're the poor kid whose parents own the local hardware store. You can't afford the legal fees and everyone knows you'd let the team run a fucking train to save your brother." I cringe at his reference. "You have till game night, get it done or this shit goes public and it will give me great satisfaction to send it to your brother and daddy myself." The line goes dead. I stand here gripping my phone in a vice-like grip, tears building at the back of my eyes. I will them away not wanting to go home with tear-stained cheeks and red-rimmed eyes. I take deep breaths and try to convince myself I'm doing this to save my family,

Corvin and myself the shame of this going public. If it did, people from back home would boycott my parents' business and Corvin would be shunned from his peers. He would no longer be the king of CHU, he would be the *whore's* brother.

I give myself another minute to wallow in self-pity before I pull it together. Straightening my shoulders, I try as hard as I can to plaster on a smile. The fake charade lasts a whole second before it falls away and the first tear falls. Once they start they don't stop. I run the rest of the way home, making it in a few minutes. I take the porch steps two at a time, push the front door open and slam it closed before racing for the stairs.

Beck and Darius both jump to their feet as I pass the living room, but I don't stop when they call my name. I run to my room where I can break down without anyone seeing me fall apart. I'm a horrible person! I slam my door closed and lock it, drop my bag and head straight for the shower. I lock Darius's side of the bathroom and strip off, then turn the water to scalding hot as a form of punishment for myself. I let the sobs tear out of me now, knowing the sound of the shower will mask them and stop the guys from hearing me fall apart. I slide down the wall and wrap my arms around my legs as I bury my face in the top and cry.

I've never let myself feel the full weight of what happened —the demand placed upon me by the person who I trusted and he fucking used me!

I let myself feel everything—all the pain, anger, shame and self-loathing. I thought running away would fix every-thing but it didn't. I was just a tool for him to use to get back at my brother and the guys, and the worst fucking part is I had no idea it happened until years fucking later!

Two years ago my whole fucking world stopped when Darius left me. I thought I was slowly healing from the loss of him, until three months ago when I overheard a conversation that changed my whole freaking life. I climb to my feet, grab my loofah and begin to scrub my skin, feeling so dirty and used!

.

CHAPTER THIRTEEN

Darius

"What the fuck?" I say aloud, confused as hell why Leah just ran through the house crying.

"Someone is going to pay for this!' Beck growls, and I nod my agreement. "What do we do, Corv isn't here?" I exhale loudly and turn to face him. His face is a mask of pure fury, fists clenched at his sides, while he stands there vibrating with anger.

"Beck?" He pulls his angry stare from the stairs Leah just ran up to look at me.

"What?"

"I need to make sure she's okay." His eyes narrow as he says,

"No, I told you—"

"Something fucking happened, Beckett. Leah doesn't cry, so whatever happened is fucking big. She needs me," I shout. His gaze hardens the longer he stands there staring at me, it takes an age before he gives me a curt nod. I'm racing out of the living room and taking the steps two at a time as I go in search of the girl that I planned to destroy, only by the looks of things, some other motherfucker beat me to it!

I grip her door handle and try to open it, but it's locked. I pound on the door for a minute but when she doesn't answer, I growl, turn and storm into my room to find the bathroom door closed. I try to open it but it's locked. Fuck this. I storm over to my desk, yank the draw open and grab my pocketknife out. I use it to twist the lock on the sliding door open. When it clicks, I chuck the knife onto my bed and open the door. Steam hits me right in the face, and the second it clears, I see her and my chest caves in.

"Fuck!" I growl as I storm into the room, and yank the glass door open. She's too focused or in a trance to even notice me thanks to her rabidly scrubbing her body. Her skin is bright red and raw from the hot water and her frantic need to scrub the skin from her body. Reaching in to turn the water off, I curse when the water splashes onto my arm—the fucking shower is hot as fuck.

I turn it off and it's only then she snaps out of it and snaps her gaze to me. Her green eyes are wide but not from fright, it's… guilt. "Goldie?" She shakes her head and takes a step back from me.

"Stay away from me, you need to get far away from me." Her voice is devoid of all emotion and that scares the shit out of me.

I raise my hands in surrender, keeping my eyes on hers as I ask, "What happened, baby?" Her bottom lip trembles and her eyes fill with tears.

"Leave, Darius!" she screams.

"Never," I growl out as I reach for her and pull her against me. She tries to fight me off but I'm too strong. I wrap my arms around her wet body as she tries to pound her little fists against my chest.

"I hate you! I fucking hate you, Darius. Let me go." I weather her words and fists for a full minute before she finally crumbles in my hold and tears pour from her eyes as she breaks down in my arms. I lift her out of the shower. She wraps her legs and arms around me as she buries her face in the crook of my neck. I snag a towel on my way out of the bathroom and head for my room. I try to place her on her feet to dry her but she won't let go. Sighing I drop down on the edge of my bed and try to dry her as best as I can before wrapping the towel around her back so she doesn't catch a chill. After a moment of hearing her sniffle and cling to me like I'm her lifeline, I give in. I wrap my arms around her and hold her tight allowing myself this moment to get lost in the feeling of being this close to her.

"I'm right here, Goldie. Whatever happened you can tell me about it," I say in a calm tone. She shakes her head against my neck and burrows in deeper, her legs locking around my waist as she tightens her grip with her arms. I've never seen Leah like this before. She is usually so fucking strong and resilient, nothing can keep this girl down. A shiver works its way through her body. I curse before I stand, her hold on me is so tight I don't even need to hold her, then pull the covers on my bed back, ready to place her underneath them but the sound of Beckett's voice has me pausing. I'm fucking glad I have my back to him or I'd have to knock my best friend out for seeing my girl naked.

My girl?

"Is she okay?" I can't even turn my head to look over my shoulder at him, thanks to the head currently buried into the side of my neck.

"She will be, now fuck off," I say in a hurried tone.

"Why is there a towel... oh fucking hell, Darius!" he snarls, and I cut in before he continues down the path of his wayward thoughts.

"I had to help her out of the shower. That's it, nothing more. Now get the fuck out so I can put her to bed," I snarl, getting annoyed at his constant intrusion into everything I do with Leah.

"Her room is next door!" he adds smugly.

"Not tonight it isn't. She stays with me, so unless you want to see our best friend's sister naked and me strip down to get in behind her, you'll get the fuck out now!" He mumbles beneath his breath but it's too quiet for me to make out. The sound of my bedroom door closing has me snapping back into action and trying to place her under the covers. Even when I lay her in the bed she refuses to let go. "You need to get under the covers, Goldie."

"Don't leave me, Darius, please." The broken tone of her voice fucking spears me. I close my eyes, trying not to war within myself. After everything she has done and put me through, can I give her one night of the old me and hold her through this? A small whimper escapes her and that makes the decision for me.

"I won't leave but I need you to let go so I can get out of these wet clothes, then I'll jump in with you."

"Pinky swear?" Despite my torment I smile at her antics— she would always make me pinky swear if she didn't think I would follow through.

"Pinky swear, Goldie, now let go and hop under the covers." My words seem to put her at ease. She releases her hold on me and slips under the covers. I make quick work of stripping off my pants and shirt, then shut off the light and climb in behind her. I keep an inch of space between us. She isn't having that, she snuggles into my side. Her leg is thrown over mine and her arm lays across my stomach. I can feel her bare fucking pussy against my side and it's taking every ounce of power I have not to roll us over and sink my hardening cock inside her tight wet heat.

Silence stretches but it isn't uncomfortable, her tears have stopped and she isn't shivering anymore. I don't know if it's from being under the covers or the fact that she is plastered to my side and absorbing my body heat. She traces lazy patterns across my abs, the feeling of her hands on me is the worst form of fucking torture but I am powerless to stop her.

Girls at CHU think they need to appear easy to capture my attention. Leah never had to do anything to capture it because she had it from the moment I saw her. I may sound like a little bitch but Leah Williams was my childhood crush and my first love. I really thought she was it for me but I was so fucking wrong. A tired sigh escapes me and she tenses.

"You're going to kick me out now, aren't you?" she whispers, her breath fans across my chest causing gooseflesh to erupt all over my body. How this girl holds so much power over me still I'll never know. I open my mouth to answer but snap it closed the moment her fingers trail lower. When she reaches the waistband of my boxers, she tilts her head back and stares up at me. The only light source is the moonlight streaming in through the windows. I can see the need in her eyes. "Please." That one whispered fucking word seals my fate. I reach out, grip her chin in my hand pulling her to me. She hovers above me searching my gaze for a sign that I'm going to back out and leave her high and dry like the other night, when she doesn't see it, she smashes her lips against mine. I groan at the taste of her when she slips her tongue inside my mouth—she tastes like *home*.

She deepens the kiss as she pushes her dainty little hand inside my boxers gripping my length. I break the kiss and hiss at the feeling of having her hand wrapped around my cock. All my carefully crafted rules fly out the window. I blew my no kissing rule with her twice. Leah has never been shy when it comes to taking what she wants or telling me what she needs. She isn't like most girls, they get shy and look away while they suck your cock but not her, she holds my gaze as she strokes me. Her strokes are slow and measured but the moment her little fingers feel the pre-cum leaking from my dick, her eyes widen and gasp slips free.

"Fuck," she grits out before yanking her hand free and

moving away, I rest up on my elbows about to lose my shit at her but she throws the covers back, grips the waistband of my briefs and yanks them down, so I keep my mouth shut.

She moans at the sight of my cock. I settle back against the pillows as I wait for her to get into position to suck me off but what she does next surprises the fuck out of me. She spins around and straddles my face between her legs. I don't have time to ponder the fact she just 69'd me because she bends down and sucks my cock into the back of her throat drawing a groan of pleasure from me.

"Shit, Goldie!" I growl a second before she pushes her pussy down onto my face. I reach around and grip the globes of her ass in my hands and squeeze at the same time I push her down onto my waiting tongue. She moans around me, the vibrations from that travel up my body drawing a shudder of pleasure out. The second she deepthroats me and cups my balls in her hand, I kick up the pace and suck her enlarged clit into my mouth. If she keeps sucking me like that I'm going to be coming down her throat and not in her pussy. I lick my way down to her opening and push my tongue inside her wet hole. Her taste assaults me and fuck if it isn't the best thing I have tasted in fucking years.

She releases my cock with a wet pop. "Oh my God, just like that." She moans as she begins to grind back and forward along my tongue, chasing her release. She grips my dick in her hand and strokes it in sync with her thrusts. After a minute, her moans begin to grow louder, her strokes become jerky and erratic. As she gets closer to her release, she drops my cock and leaps off me. Before a protest can form in my mind, she turns around and straddles me but this time, facing me. Her eyes hold mine as I suck her clit into my mouth, she throws her head back moaning my name.

"Play with my nipples," she breathes out. I do as she commands and relish in the sounds that come from her. "Oh God, hold your tongue out like that and let me ride it." I do as she demands and let her ride my fucking face loving that she is taking exactly what she wants from me. Looking up her flushed cheeks and watching her tits bounce as she fucks my face is one of the hottest sights I have ever seen. "Yes, Halfback, like that, baby, just like that," she cries out. I grip her waist and hold her in place as I quicken my pace and eat her fucking cunt like it's the last thing I will ever do. She grips my hair in her hand and pulls my face in closer. "I'm coming, don't stop." She moans, in the next second her head is thrown back as she screams my name loud enough for Beckett to hear and know what we are up to. Shudders wrack her body, my cock is so fucking hard it's painful.

I don't bring her down gently, I push her off me and climb on top. She grips my cheeks and pulls me down to her so she can kiss me. When she tastes herself on my tongue she moans. I pull back and reach into the drawer of my side table, grab a foil packet out, then tear it open with my teeth. I slide the condom on, hissing, I'm so fucking horny and ready to fuck the shit out of her.

I grip my cock and slide it through her folds relishing the sounds that come from her, she looks so beautiful beneath me. Hair wild and splayed over the bed, cheeks flushed and eyes glassy from her climax.

"I need you," she says, that's all it takes for my restraint to snap and I line my cock up with her opening. She tenses when I push the head of my cock inside her. I grit my teeth, fuck she is so tight!

"When was the last time you had sex?" I grit out through clenched teeth, she shakes her head.

"I don't want to talk about it," she says breathless. A sheen of sweat dots my forehead as I push inside her slowly not wanting to hurt her but also putting myself through fucking pain going this slow. "Fuck," she moans out when I'm halfway inside her. "I forgot how big you were." Those words have a smile breaking free on my face.

"I need to be all the way inside you, can you take it?" The strain in my voice can be heard.

"Do it, I want all of you," she says. We both cry out in pleasure and pain, I drop to my elbows on either side of her head as I wait for her to adjust to me. She breathes through her nose trying to calm herself.

"Kiss me, baby," I say in the hopes it will distract her from the pain. She obliges me and within seconds she begins to relax enough for me to move inside her.

"Oh shit," she moans against my mouth. I slowly move in and out of her, loving how she fucking fits me like a glove. I push up to rest on my haunches, grab each of her ankles and place them on either of my shoulders, as I push forward until her knees are against her chest. Leah being a dancer has always benefited me when it came to the bedroom—the girl is so flexible and willing to allow me to bend her any way I like. I draw my cock out, leaving only the head inside her before slamming back in. We both cry out as pleasure ripples through our body. I can't draw this out, I have wanted this for too fucking long. I'll make it up to her later.

"I can't go slow, I need to fuck you and come so badly," I say in a clipped tone.

"Fuck me and make me scream your name." I do as commanded, and fuck her so hard her legs wind up being flat against her chest. When her cries become too loud, I slam my lips against hers to quiet her down. She tries to break the kiss but I don't let her as I continue to pound inside her fucking pussy chasing my own release. She bites down on my bottom lip, making my eyes blaze with desire as I stare down at the little minx. She releases my lip, reaches around her legs and cups my face. "I'm gonna come," she whispers. Her brows dip and then she is arching off the bed screaming my name. I feel my balls tightening and know I'm a second away from joining her in ecstasy. Three more pumps inside her and my head is thrown back as I roar out my release.

I've never fucked anyone but Leah front on and I sure as shit have never tasted another pussy on my tongue except hers. We were each other's firsts and in a lot of ways I may have cut her from my life but I still couldn't allow myself to tarnish what we shared by giving that part of myself to someone else.

CHAPTER FOURTEEN

Leah

Darius and I are panting, breathless from the best sex of my life and grateful Corvin wasn't here to hear me screaming his best friend's name as he made come all over his glorious cock.

"I need to pull out." I nod and bite down on my bottom to brace myself for the pain that will follow. I whimper when he pulls out and I feel the sting. "Shit, I'm sorry." He slips off the bed and my heart sinks, he's going to kick me out. I watch his retreating form head into the bathroom, then I gather what pride I have left and slide off the bed. I snag a black shirt off the floor and try to pull it on, but freeze when I get it over my head at the sound of his angry tone.

"What the fuck are you doing?" I stare at him confused. He stands naked and proud. My gaze drops to his cock and my mouth waters, wanting to taste him again. Sucking Darius off is one of my favorite things to do. "Leah!" he snaps. I shake my head to clear my thoughts.

"I thought you would want me to leave because… well… I mean you need to—"

"Get in the fucking bed, Leah. You're not going anywhere," he snaps as he makes his way back to me. I turn and frown at him as he slips beneath the covers and pulls the other side back for me. I move toward him ready to hold him while I sleep. "Lose the fucking shirt. You know the rules, no clothes when you sleep with me." I can't stop the goofy grin from stretching across my face. I do as he says and yank the shirt off before slipping in beside him. His arms encircle me, while I lay my head against his naked chest and breathe him in. I miss this.

I miss him.

I want to ask him what happened between us and why he left me but I'm also scared as hell to hear his answer. What if it was because I wasn't good enough. Was I shit in bed? Too clingy? Memories of the last time we were together run through my mind. We had a fight before his game. I was tired of sneaking around and being his little secret. I wanted him to tell Corvin about us. He said my brother wouldn't understand because he was eighteen and I was sixteen at the time. I didn't care about age, I just wanted Darius to tell Corv that I was his and there wasn't a thing my brother could do about it.

Except he didn't.

He said it wasn't the right time and to go home and wait for him to get there. I didn't listen. Saint told me they had a party to go to after the game. I decided if he wouldn't tell Corvin, then I would at the party, except I never saw him again after that night. Something worse happened and I wish every day for the past three months that I had listened and went straight home like I was told.

"Darius–" I try to speak but he cuts me off.

"Not tonight, Leah. If we go down that path we won't be sleeping in the same bed or talking to each other again. Leave the past alone for the night." I take a deep breath and try to shoot my shot, the worst he could do is turn me down so I decide to go for it.

"Can we forget the past until Monday night, when Corvin gets home, then we can go back to normal?" I can hear the pleading tone in my own voice but I don't care. If four days is all he'll give me then I'll take them.

Fuck, who am I kidding?

I'll take anything Darius gives me because I'm still in love with the boy who stole my heart years ago.

"That's not a good idea," he rushes out but I know Darius, the tone of his voice and how he went rigid tells me he wants this too.

"It's four days. After that you can go back to acting like you hate me when I know you don't."

"I do hate you!" he growls, and I roll my eyes, even though he can't see me.

"I'll pretend like I believe you and we can also pretend that your cock isn't getting hard right now at the thought of being able to fuck me whenever and wherever you like because my brother isn't here." My words are his undoing, in a split second I'm on my back with my tall, dark and handsome bad boy looming above me. I reach up to touch him but he grips my wrists in each of his hands and pins them on either side of my head. Not one to go down without a fight, I open my legs wider and thrust my hips upward, then smile triumphantly when I feel his hard cock brush against my pussy. "Who's the liar now?" I taunt. His eyes darken but in the most delicious way. I know that look and it means Darius is going to fuck me into submission until I tell him I was wrong and he was right, even when he wasn't.

"You know I'm gonna make you take that back, right?" The husky tone of his voice has my fucking pussy fluttering! I lock my legs around his waist and pull him down to me, gasping when I feel the tip of his cock push against my entrance, his eyes blaze with need.

"Give me these four days and I'll let you do whatever you

want to me. I'll take them back right now if you give in." I can't keep the desperation out of my voice even if I tried. I need this and I know he does too. We can work everything else out on Tuesday but for now, I just want to let our bodies do the talking and fool myself into thinking that Darius could somehow be mine one day. That will never happen after I do what I have to do, but four days with him means I'll finally be able to let him go and in my own weird way, say goodbye.

"Four days," he says as he slowly pushes inside me, drawing a moan from deep within my chest. "Wherever and whenever I want. You deny me once and the deal is off, got it?"

"Yes," I moan.

"I want to fuck in the living room while Beckett is next to us, you gonna say no?" he asks just as he buries himself fully inside me, I moan. "Answer me," he snaps as he begins to thrust in and out of me lazily.

"No, I'll fuck you in front of him whatever you want, just don't stop moving, please!" He places a quick kiss to the tip of my nose before saying,

"Good girl." His thrust grows harder and deeper—fuck he feels so good inside me! He releases his hold on my wrists, rests back on his haunches then pulls me up so I'm sitting on top of him. I look at him and my heart lurches to life at the sight of this God beneath me. I wrap my arms around his shoulders and capture his lips in a kiss that I hope conveys everything I feel for him. "Move for me, Goldie," he rasps out, and I do just that. I glide up and down on his cock. He feels so much deeper from this angle and fuck, it feels so good. He captures my nipple in his mouth and swipes his tongue over my enlarged bud pulling a moan from me.

"Bite it!" I demand. He clamps his teeth on my nipple and that's it, I cry out as my pussy clenches his cock trying to milk it of its cum as I come all over his cock.

"That's it baby, ride me while you come." Shudders wrack

my body as I come down from my high. He places a soft kiss to my lips before maneuvering us so he is once again on top of me. Unlike last time, he doesn't rush. He takes his time sliding in and out of me, making sure I can feel every glorious inch of him. His hands cup either side of my face as he bends down, I expect him to kiss me but he doesn't, he holds my stare as he makes… love to me.

Moisture gathers in the corners of my eyes. Darius may not be able to say it with words but he is saying it with his body, he loves me but something from our past still haunts him to the point he can't let me in.

My emotions get the better of me, before I can stop them the words fly out of my mouth. "I love you." My eyes widen but I don't regret saying them because they are true. He doesn't miss a beat, his pace remains the same and his expression doesn't change as he speaks.

"I know you do, Goldie," is all he says before he kisses me. Questions swirl through my mind and I feel hurt but what did I expect? For him to say it back? All thought flees my body when he pushes deeper inside me, drawing a long deep moan from me, he breaks the kiss and buries his face in the side of my neck. He sucks my flesh into his mouth while he fucks me, and his pace begins to quicken.

"Oh God, like that," I say, he keeps the same pace and intensity, a minute goes by and my pussy clamps down on his cock.

"Fuck yes, come with me, baby," he growls out, gives two more pumps and then we are both flying over the edge into euphoric bliss. My pussy is greedy and clamping down on him, not wanting him to ever leave. I have to agree with her. But the moment he pulls out of me he rests his hands on the tops of my knees, pushes my legs open wider and smiles possessively. "Fuck, do you know how good you look with my cum dripping out of you?" My eyes open so wide they begin to hurt.

"What the fuck! You didn't put a condom on?" He shoots me a condescending look.

"You were the one who pulled my cock into *you!*" I roll my eyes.

"How do I know you didn't catch anything from that ratty bitch you had over?" His brows hit his hairline and it pisses me off when I see him trying to fight his smile from breaking free. "I'm serious, this isn't funny!" I snap.

"So, you're more worried you caught herpes than you are that you might be pregnant?" I glare up at him, also fully aware I am naked and have his cum currently dripping out of me. I feel it sliding into my ass and fight the shudder that wants to break free. Darius doesn't miss a beat, running his finger through my folds, capturing his cum and pushing it back inside me. I can't help the moan that breaks free. "My cum belongs inside you," he says as he pulls his finger out and smears it over my stomach. "And on you." His words shouldn't turn me on but they fucking do. As if he has a direct link to my pussy, it clamps down trying to hold his cum inside me.

To distract myself from thoughts of him fucking me again and coming in my mouth I answer his question. "I'm on the pill and have been since I was fourteen, remember? It helps control the flow of my periods." He smirks and nods, motherfucker. "You remembered?" He quirks a brow at me.

"I've never fucked a girl without a condom, Leah, and I also never fucked Chelsea. You are the only one and of course I remembered. I would never take an uncalculated risk like that." Embarrassment washes over me, his features soften at the sight. "Come on, we need to clean you up so I can fill you up again." I frown at him in confusion and he rolls his eyes playfully. "We're going to wash my cum out of your beautiful cunt then I'm going to fuck you in the shower and fill you up. Tonight, you will wear panties to bed so I know my cum will stay right where it belongs."

I fucking moan at his dirty depraved words. I can't lie to myself though, it has always been a turn on for me seeing Darius get all possessive and alpha male. Some women hate it but I'm not one of them. When he slips off the bed and offers me his hand, I take it without hesitation, excited for him to ruin me over the next four days before *I* ruin him.

CHAPTER FIFTEEN

Darius

I sip my protein shake and lean over the railing on the back porch as I watch Leah, Katie and Cody practice their dance. I don't know what the fuck any of the moves are called but I do know Leah looks fucking good doing them. The three girls are standing around in a makeshift circle having a water break. Leah throws her head back and laughs at something Katie says. I watch her body tense and her laughter die off as she peers over shoulder at me. I smirk, I knew she would feel me watching her. She always said that she could pick me out in a room full of people blindfolded. What she doesn't know is the same goes for me. Her eyes twinkle in delight at the sight of me shirtless and wearing low-slung basketball shorts.

She's going to pay for letting me wake up to an empty bed. I'll admit, the moment I woke up and felt her side empty I panicked until I heard laughter and peeked out the window to see her outside with her friends. I decided to work out in the basement while she trained. We didn't get much sleep last night but fuck, I've never felt so alive. She shoots me a wink before turning back to her friends who both shoot her a knowing look. She shrugs and the three of them laugh before dropping their drinks and getting ready to go another round.

"You're playing with fire." My shoulders slump and my good mood sours at the sound of Beckett's voice. I know he is only trying to watch out for Corvin and me in his own way but I'm a big boy and know what I'm doing. He slides up beside me and mimics my position, but instead of a protein shake, he sips a coffee. When I see him in a pair of sweats and shirtless, I quirk a brow.

"I know you didn't work out, which means your lack of dress is because you just walked your pussy out the front door." He pins me with a dirty look, I return it.

"At least she wasn't one of our best friend's sisters." I grimace, then turn back to watch the girls as they slowly lower themselves to the ground and then push their hips up and down while punching the ground, it looks fucking hot. "Stay away from her." I look back to Beckett and shake my head.

"We agreed, her and I have until Monday night when Corv gets back. Give me this, Beckett, Corvin will never know," I plead.

"She isn't some random girl, Darius. She is part of our... family."

"You don't think I know that?" I snap. "I wish she wasn't his sister but I can't help that I lo..." I clamp my mouth closed and curse as I turn away from him, drop my glass on the table and march over to the girls. They don't hear me coming, thanks to the music blasting from the JBL speaker. I creep up behind Leah and wrap my arms around her waist. She screams in surprise but I don't allow her to recover as I spin and rush toward the pool.

"Darius, no!" she shouts but it's too late, we're already soaring through the air then crash through the surface of the water. She pushes away from me as she swims to the surface. I break the surface and laugh at the angry look on her face. "You are such a dick!" Her words pack no heat, so I swim over to her and push the loose strands of hair from her face, grip her waist and lift her. She wraps her arms and legs around me as she melts into my hold.

"You looked hot, I thought I would help you cool off." She throws her head back and laughs.

"You are such a dork," she says with a smile. I press a chaste kiss to her lips and shoot her a wink.

"Throwing you in the pool was my form of revenge for letting me wake up alone!" Her features soften and now she is the one placing a kiss to my lips. She pulls back and ghosts her lips over mine.

"I'll make it up to you tonight." I growl my approval, but before I can kiss her again, she turns to her friends and waves them over.

"Leah, I think I just got pregnant from watching that display of raw sexual need." Leah and Cody both break out into a full-on belly laugh at their friend's crazy ass. At the sound of pounding footfalls. I snap my gaze to the other side, but I'm too late to cover my face from the splash as Beck leaps through the air yelling.

"Toron Amo!"

"Motherfucker!" I snarl as water drips down my face. Leah laughs and wipes the water off my face, kisses me once more before wigging free of my hold to go hang with her friends. I've decided at this moment, I don't like her friends, they are taking up too much of *my* time. All her time should be spent with me, not them.

"Glare any harder and your face will crack." The sarcasm is thick in Beck's voice, which just grates on my fucking nerves.

"Shut up," I snap as I swim to the other side of the pool. Beck follows and we lean against the edge and watch the girls laugh and splash each other. Seeing Leah happy brings a smile to my face. The longer I look at her, the more I wonder, how am I going to let her go?

"You need to end whatever this is before it goes too far." I lull my head to the side and stare at Beck. His gaze is on the girls. I study him for a moment and watch as a small smile twitches at the corner of his mouth when Leah begins to laugh at something Cody said. My eyes widen as I push off the wall to block his line of sight. He frowns when he sees the look on my face, I can't fucking believe this. "What?"

I shake my head annoyed at myself for not seeing this earlier, how the fuck could I have missed it? "You noticed everything about what I was up to with Leah years ago because *you* were watching her too! You care so much about what I do to her because *you* want to be the one doing it to her as well." Beckett's face hardens, his upper lip pulls back in snarl. "Now, how long have you been in love with *my* girl?" He pushes off the wall of the pool and gets right in my face, pushing his forehead into mine. The conversation behind us stops as the girls focus their attention on us.

"You don't know what the fuck you are talking about," he seethes.

"Why the fuck do you care so much if you don't have feelings for her, big man?" I taunt, his gaze searches mine for a second.

"Fuck you, Darius, you stay the hell out of my business!"

"I'll stay out of yours if you stay the fuck out of mine and Leah's. You think you can get her to notice you?" I scoff like an arrogant son of a bitch before continuing. "I've always been the center of her world and her attention will always be on me. You will never have a chance where she is concerned."

"You are such an asshole!" I spin away from Beck to see Leah and the other two girls looking at us with looks of disgust, anger and the one that cuts me deep is the look of betrayal on Leah's face. I push away from Beck to go to her but the three of them scramble to get out of the pool and away from me. I reach the edge of the pool, grip the side ready to jump out but the look she pins me with has me pausing. "I don't know what is worse, the fact that I can let a guy who ghosted me for years back into my bed without thought, or the fact that I was stupid enough to ever believe that you would ever see me as anything more than your dirty little secret." I grind my teeth so hard they begin to ache. She thinks she can stand there and look down her nose at me after what she fucking did!

I push out of the pool, move into her space until my chest is against her. She cranes her neck back to meet my angry stare. My fists clench and unclench at my sides as I battle within myself to try calm the anger that is coursing through my body like wildfire. The sound of Beckett getting out of the pool and heading around to us makes the decision for me, my anger wins out.

"You stand there like you're the perfect fucking Virgin Mary and yet you're the whole fucking reason I do what I do now!" I scream in her face. She stumbles back a step with wide eyes, fear flashes through them. "Miss fucking perfect thinks she can come *here* to *my* house and have a right to be pissy with me?" I laugh but there is no humor to it. I close the space between us again, grip the back of her neck, bending down so we are eye level, then deliver the final blow that I know will break her. "I knew fucking you again would be easy because a girl like you spreads her legs for anyone." Her hand strikes out so fast I don't have time to block the hit. My cheek stings from her hit but I don't try to soothe the ache. Her gaze spears me, her green eyes burn with hatred.

"You love to call me a slut and whore but let's not forget who is the one with the track record here, *halfback*." Hearing my old pet name from her roll off her tongue with such venom has me stilling. "I never left you for anyone, you left me, remember?" I push in closer until the tips of our noses are touching. I can feel her breath fanning across my lips.

"Nah, you just like to get fucked at a party by my worst enemy because you're a deceitful bitch like that and like to play offside, don't you, Goldie?" Her eyes are so wide they remind me of dinner plates. I pull back and stare down at her pale face and shake my head in disgust when tears fill her eyes as her body begins to tremble. "Oh, baby, don't act so shocked. You didn't really think you were different, did you?" I tsk like an asshole. "Goldie, you were a phase, the forbidden fruit if you will and fuck, did I love destroying your innocence," I say as I bite my lip and run my gaze up and down her body. "But now, you're nothing but a used up, cum dumpster for the team to hit when they feel the need."

I expect her to fight back, scream, shout, or even hit me but what I don't expect is for a gut-wrenching sob to tear from her as tears pour down her cheeks before she takes off... running. I watch as she runs through the gate around the side of the house, soaking wet with her two friends chasing after her and shouting her name, for her to come back. My breaths are coming in short rapid pants as my anger continues to ride me. She fucking had it coming! I repeat that over and over in my mind until a pissed off looking Beckett comes into view.

"Go," I snap and do a shooing motion with my hand. "Go chase after her and be her savior. Now's your chance to finally nail her, Beck. Believe me, bro, the girl can suck dick better than *Jesse James*." The words have barely left my mouth before his fist connects with my jaw, sending me sailing through the air and crashing through the surface of the pool water. I push off the bottom of the pool and swim to the top, the moment I break the surface his angry shouts await me.

"I don't like her like that. Leah reminds me of someone I fucking lost, you dumb fuck!" My brows raise, I've never heard Beck talk about someone from his past before. "You think she cheated on you, is that it?"

"Stay out of it," I growl.

"You're a fucking pussy, Darius. Leah is everything you aren't. That girl has loved you since she was a child. Anyone with fucking eyes can see it. How Corvin hasn't noticed beats me. You are a fucking idiot. Just to clarify shit for you because you're a fucking dumbass, I am going after Leah, but it isn't to get in her pants. It is to make sure our best friend's little sister is okay!" Before I can think of a witty retort he is running toward the house. I punch the water and growl out in frustration, fucking Leah! The girl is like a poison I can't seem to get out of my fucking system. Truth is, I don't know if I want her out of my system.

CHAPTER SIXTEEN

Leah

I don't know where I'm running to, Cody and Katie gave up chasing me a while ago and I'm grateful for that. I couldn't face them after knowing they heard what Darius just said to me, his words cutting me deeper than he will ever know.

He knew.

He knew this whole fucking time and never once said a thing. After all these years I finally found out why he disappeared from my life. I slipped into the worst depression after I found out what happened to me. I couldn't claw my fucking way out of that dark hole. I can feel the claws of my depression trying to drag me under again, only this time, I don't think I have the strength to pull myself out knowing that Darius thinks I wanted what happened.

I slam to a stop when I realize I've found my way to the beach. I trek out to the bank and drop down allowing the sobs to claw their way out of me. The sea breeze sends a chill down my spine thanks to my soaked clothes. I try with all my might to stay out of my head and soak in the beauty around me. The beach is empty and the only sounds that can be heard are the waves crashing against the shore, the ocean is so beautiful and yet equal parts deadly. The beauty of the ocean can lull anyone into thinking that they can master it and control it but the truth is, the ocean is like a heart. No matter how hard you tell the organ to stop feeling what it does, it never listens because love is the same as the sea—equal parts beautiful and deadly.

⬩

When I feel arms lift me, I snap my eyes open ready to scream until I look up and see his face. My heart breaks at the sight of him. I dart my gaze around and that's when I realize night has fallen, I must have fallen asleep! A shiver works its way through my body, making me realize that I'm freezing. He curses beneath his breath and quickens his pace.

"I got her!" Darius shouts. I lull my head to the side to see headlights in the parking lot. "Turn up the heat, she's freezing." I close my eyes not wanting to see his face, how can he come find me asleep on the beach, act like he cares when he and I both know he hates me. "I don't hate you, Leah." His clipped tone has me snapping my gaze open and cursing under my breath for speaking my thoughts out loud. When we reach the car, I see Beck standing there with a sad smile on his face holding the passenger door open for me. Instead of putting me in the seat like I thought he would, he slips in with me still in his hold. I try to wiggle free but his hold around my waist tightens. I maneuver myself so I'm sitting on his lap rather than being held bride style. Beck closes the door and moves to the other side. I hold my hands out in front of the vent and sigh when I feel the heat starting to thaw my frozen fingers.

Beck slips into the driver seat of his car, puts it in drive and peels out of the lot. The tension in the car is palpable but I refuse to speak, I already feel uncomfortable at the fact I'm sitting on Darius's lap rather than on the actual seat. I sigh in relief when I see the two-story I have now come to call home until my dorm building is ready. The moment Beck puts the car in park, I grab the handle and push the door open. I nearly fall flat on my face trying to escape Darius but I don't care. I steady myself and hold my head high as I march toward the house ready to take the longest, hottest shower in the history of showers.

"Unless you're hiding a key in that sports bra, the doors locked." I freeze on the second step, then inhale a deep breath as I turn back toward the two assholes who are leaning against the car with smug looks on their faces. Darius holds his keys out to me. "Give me a kiss and I'll unlock it for you." I keep my face blank and I make my way down the stairs, the self-satisfied smirk on his face makes what I'm about to do so much sweeter. I stop two steps away from him, bend down and grab a rock. Beck and Darius's eyes are wide. I spin on my heel, march up the stairs and peg the rock through one of the windows on one side of the door. "What the fuck."

"Leah!"

They both shout at the same time, I turn my head to the side and shoot them both a wink as I carefully go through the *new* front door I made and make my way upstairs, ignoring the pair of them calling for me. They can sort out the fucking window. It's the least Darius can do after the shit he put me through today! I don't even bother to lock his side of the bathroom knowing he'll just break in again like he did last night. I kick off my sneakers and cringe at the feeling of having soggy socks on, knowing my feet will look like prunes. My clothes are next to go. Dumping them into the hamper in the corner, I step into the shower stall and switch the faucet to hot. I step back and give it time to heat up before I'm stepping under the spray and allowing it to wash away the pain and aches of the worst fucking day.

How I went from waking smiling with Darius beside me, to him flipping out and saying such horrid things to me is confusing as fuck. I need to learn that Darius and I are doomed, we will never be more than shared kisses in the dark corner of the room. We will never be a couple and happily in love. We are destined to be apart. If I could just find the courage to tell him, then maybe he would understand but in order to tell him the truth that means I expose myself to my stupidity and the fact that I should have listened to him and just stayed the fuck home!

After shaving and washing my hair and body, I flick the shower off and step out onto the bath mat only to realize I forgot to grab my towel. Shit! I wring my hair out as best I can as I make my way into my bedroom, I just want to hop into my *Oodie* and snuggle up in bed for the rest of the night.

"Jesus Christ!"

"Close your fucking eyes!" I snap my wide-eyed gaze to my bedroom door, to see both Beckett and Darius standing there. When Becks gaze lands on me, he slams his eyes closed like Darius commanded. I ignore the heated look in Darius's eyes as I roll mine in return. "Put some fucking clothes on!" I keep my back to them and fight the smile from breaking free when I bend over and grab my towel off the ground next to my bed. The sharp intake of breath tells me Darius got a good eyeful of my pussy. "I'm not fucking with you, Leah!"

I snort as I wrap the towel around my head, turn back to them both–still naked–then place my hands on my hips. I dart my gaze between them both. I can see from the strain on Beck's forehead he is trying so hard not to let his gaze drop lower. I shoot him a wink before looking back to a seething Darius, his face taut with tension, fists clenched at his sides.

"For someone who continues to call me a slut daily, you are mighty concerned about who happens to see me naked." My voice is breathy and sounds sexy to my own ears. Darius's eyes blaze with heat but there in the depths of his brown eyes I can see fury lurking. Beck, on the other hand, just looks stunned. Fuck it, I'm gonna play this out. Knowing both their gazes are on me, I move toward the dresser and pull open my panty drawer. I keep my back to them as I fish out my black lace thong, then bend and relish in the hisses that I hear coming from behind me.

"Close your fucking eyes!" Darius shouts. "Better yet, fuck off, Beckett!" I pull my thong up and just to drive my point home, I stretch out the pencil-thin elastic on the sides and let it snap into place. I grab the matching bra and spin around to face both guys as I slowly put my bra on. I cock my head to the side, loving how my body can have both these guys' attention so captivated.

"I never picked either of you two for being voyeurs." Darius growls, warning me not to push this. Fuck him. I clip my bra into place, remove the towel from my head and shake out my long blonde hair before sauntering over to them. I can feel Darius's heated stare drinking in every exposed inch of my nakedness. He smirks, thinking I'm going for him, but at the last second I turn to Beck. He gulps as a gleeful feeling erupts inside me knowing I have the both of them eating out of the palm of my hand. Good, because Darius is going to see what it feels like to be hurt!

"Darius and I have had sex in *a lot* of places but my favorites are the places where there is a chance we could get caught, you know the whole thrill of it." I dart my tongue out and suck my bottom lip into my mouth to drive my point home, knowing they are both watching my every move. "It really turns me on!" I barely get the last word out before Darius has me swung over his shoulder caveman style and landing a swift slap to my ass that has me squealing.

"Your fucking show is done! Beckett get the fuck out!"

I cut the arrogant bastard off. "No, Beck, stay! If Darius wants to fuck me like the whore I am why not watch, shit I might even let you run a fucking train!" I scream in anger. Darius throws me off his shoulder. I squeak in surprise when I land on my bed, and two seconds later he is on top of me, pinning my arms on either side of my head as he glares down at me. I return his angry look with one of my own.

"You think this is fucking funny?" he snarls bending so we are nose to nose.

"I thought this is what you wanted?" The confused look that mars his beautiful face pisses me off. "Let me spell it the fuck out for you, Halfback. I never let a team run a fucking train. I never let anyone touch me–" I feel the lump start to form in my throat, tears build in the back of my eyes but I fight through it. "The only person I ever wanted or let touch me was you. Now, get the fuck off me so I can pack my shit because I'm done." The stunned look on his face would be comical if I wasn't fighting with everything I had to not cry in front of him and Beck. I try to push him off me but he's too lost in his own head, trying to decipher my words.

"Show him." I stop fighting and turn my head to the side to see Beck now stands a foot away from my bed with a look of... lust in his eyes. Lust? There is no freaking way Beckett Dawson finds me attractive, is there? He drops his gaze to me and the intensity in his pale green eyes has my breath hitching. "Show him you only want him, with me standing right here." I hold his stare for a second before slowly looking back at Darius, who is frowning down at me. I don't know what the hell is going on and I am so confused.

"Do you want him?" The husky tone of Darius's voice has need building inside me. What the fuck is wrong with me, he was cruel and mean today and here I am beneath him getting wet just from the tone of his voice. Unsure on how to answer him, I turn away. He grips my chin and forces my gaze back to him, the intensity in it has my body warming and my chest feeling tight. "Answer me, Goldie."

"I... I don't..." I can't even form a coherent sentence. I only want Darius but the thought of living out a fantasy with Darius and Beck is hard to deny. I trust both of these men to care for me and keep me safe, which is why it's hard to say *no*. Darius bends down and runs his nose along the column of my neck to my lobe before clamping his teeth gently. Despite me trying not to, a moan still slips free. His hot breath fans across my ear, sending a shiver down my spine and my eyes rolling back. Darius has always had a way of making me forgive him just from the way he can play my body like an instrument.

"I want you, Goldie." His whispered words are my undoing, all thoughts of Beckett fly out the window when I cup Darius's face and pull his lips to mine. The moment my tongue pushes through his lips, he groans at the taste of me. I know this is so fucked up and isn't healthy, I just don't care. He may never be mine publicly but a huge part of me will always belong to him and I came to terms with that a long time ago. He deepens the kiss as he grinds his growing erection into me. I gasp into his mouth granting him full access that he takes advantage of. He becomes my oxygen, he has the ability to suck the life out of me only to breathe it back into my lungs.

CHAPTER SEVENTEEN

Darius

The anger I felt toward her earlier has vanished as I lose myself in the kiss. Beck and I had searched for her for hours. Cody and Katie had no idea where she went and it was then I remembered her love of the ocean. The sight of her tucked into a ball asleep on the beach killed me—I hate that I can't hate her!

Seeing her parade around her room naked with Beckett watching had a rage I never felt before come to life inside me. I wanted to tear his eyes out for seeing *my* girl naked but watching the way her eyes blazed at having both of us staring at her, wanting her had my cock hardening. I break the kiss and stare down at her, both of us are panting and gasping for air. Her cheeks are flushed, eyes bright and glassy unlike earlier when they were devoid of all emotion except heartbreak.

If I'm to give her the four days like she asked then I need to let the past go for now. The only bonus is, come Monday night when Corv gets back, I know I will be able to let her walk away. All I have to think about is what she did and the anger makes all the want, need and... love I feel for her evaporate in an instant. I search her gaze for a second before flicking my eyes to Beck to see him standing there stiff and struggling with what to do next.

Can I share her with him?

I find her trying so hard not to allow her eyes to stray toward him. I know they care about each other but she doesn't feel for him what she does for me, and having both Beck and I would be an experience she could check off her bucket list. Yes, that is a thing. She has a list and told me about it when we were together, one of those things was having a threesome with me and another guy. I never thought I would ever consider it until *now*.

"If we do this," I say drawing her attention to me, "I call the shots, you don't argue and do everything I say, got it?" She bites her bottom lip as her little nose scrunches up, uncertainty clouds her features.

"Will you hold this against me?" Her quietly asked question has a smile tugging at the corner of my lips.

"No. But this will be a one-time thing," I say as I look from her to him. She swallows loudly as she slowly lifts her gaze to Beck. Whether she notices or not, her hands grip my forearms in a way that has me filled with pride that she knows even if I'm angry, I'll always protect her.

"D-do you want this?" she asks Beck hesitantly. Rather than use words, the big fucker sits on the edge of the bed next to us. He reaches out and brushes his knuckles over her cheek, a blush begins to form where his knuckles touch. The thought of someone else touching her has always sent me spiraling, but watching Beckett touch her, it has a whole new sensation of feelings soaring to life inside me.

"Yes." His quietly spoken word has her eyes darkening and her chest rising and falling faster. Her bed is too small for what the three of us are planning to do. I slide off her, feeling her gaze on me the whole time. I shoot her a smile trying to ease her nerves as I offer her my hand. She hesitantly takes it, allowing me to help her to her feet. Fuck she looks gorgeous in this black lace pantie set, hair out and wild with no make-up on, she is effortlessly beautiful.

"Your beds too small, mine is bigger." A whoosh of air escapes her as I lead the three of us through the joining bathroom into my room. I release her hand and step aside allowing her to call the shots. She may think I have fucked my way through the school and had plenty of threesomes but the truth is, I have only ever had one and it was with some random girl Beck and I picked up at a party over a year ago. She takes a step forward, then another and pauses. Beckett and I stand here shoulder to shoulder shamelessly checking out her ass. Fuck, I want to smack the shit out of it and then kiss it better before pushing my cock into her tight ass.

I snap out of my thoughts when the sound of her sharp intake of breath can be heard. She reaches around her back and pops the clasp of her bra. Beck and I share a side glance before we watch silently for her next move. She chucks her bra to the side pulling a small smile from me, is it wrong that I'm proud of her for going after what she wants unlike most girls who would be too scared to admit that they want to be fucked by two guys?

She grips the sides of her thong and pushes them down her long-ass legs. A groan escapes the both of us at the sight of her bent over and her bare pussy on display. She steps free of her panties and slowly turns back to face us. I expected to see hesitation in her eyes but no trace can be found, all I see when she looks at me is trust and excitement.

"Don't hold back." Those three little words from her mouth have the both of us snapping into action. Our shirts are first to go, then the shoes and lastly, the pants. We both stand here in our briefs, hard and ready to give her the best time of her life. She runs her eyes over Beck, then she nibbles her bottom lip at the sight of his body. Before I even have the chance to feel insecure, her gaze cuts to me. When her eyes glaze over and her chest begins to rise in quick succession, all the worrying flees my body. She wants Beck but only in a physical way, when she looks at me, she wants everything I can give her physical but she also wants my fucking soul. Stupid girl, doesn't understand the meaning of soulmate.

She's my soul which is why every time I'm inside her I feel whole again. Being near her makes me feel like I'm not lost anymore, that I finally found my way home.

"Get on the bed," I order. She does as she is told but in a sexy as fuck way. She crawls up the bed offering the both of us a view of her glistening pussy that has my cock twitching at the thought of slipping inside her tight wet fucking cunt. She rests against the pillows with one leg straight and the other bent at the knee. I cock my head to the side as I watch her slowly lift her other leg, and before I can even grasp what the hell she is doing, she opens her legs at the knees giving us a front row seat to the show she is putting on. She runs her hand up the middle of her chest in a slow measured move, I swallow to try to moisten my throat when she reaches the top of her pussy. I hear Becks sharp intake of breath when she swipes a single finger through her folds. I expect her to start playing with her pussy to torture us a bit, I should know by now she doesn't ever do what I expect.

"Want a taste?" she asks in the sexiest voice I have ever heard as she holds her finger out to us. The both of us move in unison. I want to lick her finger clean but I decide to leave that taste to Beckett and go for the real thing. We stalk over to her, side by side; Beckett branches off to the side of the bed while I crawl up the bottom. The bed dips when he climbs on, and I watch with rapt attention as he reaches out, grips her tiny wrist in his hand and sucks her finger into his mouth, drawing a gasp from her. He moans at the taste before slowly releasing her finger with a wet pop, her eyes wide and filled with lust.

He doesn't take his eyes off her as he asks, "What's the boundaries, D?" Her eyes look to me. I search them for a second wondering how far I can let him go. The truth is, this is supposed to be about her but in reality, this is about me and what I am willing to allow her to do with someone else under my guidance.

I grip her thighs in a tight hold that has her squirming from the pressure of it. "Give her everything she wants until I say no." That's all he needed to hear before he bends down, gripping her face and smashing his lips against hers. I stare at them for a minute. How can I be okay with seeing her kiss my best friend, but not okay with walking in on her naked in bed with Gary?

I push those dark thoughts from my head, I won't ruin the time we have left. I slide my hands up her inner thighs, relishing in the shiver that rolls though her body at my touch. I part her pussy with my fingers before I bend down and swipe my tongue through her slick folds. A moan sounds from her but Beckett won't allow her to break the kiss. He moves one of his hands to her nipple and rolls the hardened bud between his fingers as I continue to lap at her, savoring the taste.

"You like that?" I hear Beck ask before he shifts on the bed and captures her other nipple in his mouth whilst tweaking the other with his hand, she throws her head back.

"Fuck yes," she says on a moan. I push a finger inside her tight pussy, loving the whimper that tumbles from her lips. "Oh fuck!" she cries out as I push it in and out of her while sucking her clit into my mouth at the same time. Beckett releases her nipple with a wet pop, shifts and maneuvers himself so he is sitting behind her. He reaches around her and cups both her tits in each of his hands growling his approval. I keep my gaze on them as I continue to eat her. My cock is so fucking hard just from seeing them together and how she responds to his touch.

"Watch him eat your pussy." She nods and does as he says, her eyes hooded and glazed over. "You keep your eyes open and on him when you come all over his face, do you understand?"

"Yes," she cries out, doing exactly as he says. Beckett is a dominant fucker when it comes to sex, he likes control but he knows he won't get that here tonight. Leah is mine and I call the fucking shots where she is concerned. Right now, I'll let him have his control because I want exactly what he is demanding of her. "Darius, don't stop," she cries as she arches off Beck's chest. I keep to the same pace doing *exactly* what I have been doing. Women don't want a guy to go harder or change up exactly what they are doing when they say *don't stop* or *I'm coming.* "Fuck!" she cries out a second before the walls of her pussy are clenching my finger and spasms begin to wrack her body. I gently slide my tongue up and down her slit easing her down from her high.

As the shudders roll through her, I lean back on my haunches, pull my finger free and hold it out to her. Her eyes burn with desire as she shifts forward, opens her mouth and sucks my finger clean whilst holding my gaze. When she swirls her tongue around the digit, a small moan tumbles from my lips as I envision her doing the same to my cock. Beckett brushes her hair to the side and kisses a trail down the side of her neck.

"You think you can take both of us, at once?" Beckett's whispered words have her eyes shooting wide and looking to me for reassurance. I keep my face neutral letting her dictate whether she wants this or not. I slip my finger from her mouth and wait. Her green eyes bore into mine searching for what, I have no idea.

"Yes." Desire spurs to life inside Beck's eyes. She reaches out and grips the waistband of my boxers pulling them down just enough for my cock to spring free. "But we do this my way," she says as she begins to stroke, pulling a long-drawn hiss from me. "Get on your back, I'm gonna fuck you while I suck Beck off." Her words have both of us scrambling to do as she commands. I don't take orders in the bedroom but when they are delivered by Leah, in that tone and looking at me the way she is, I'll do anything she wants.

CHAPTER EIGHTEEN

Leah

Darius lays naked on his back with his cock out, I straddle his lap and watch as Beck stands at the edge of the bed pushing his boxers down to reveal his *huge* cock. It's about the same length as Darius's but the girth on his is fucking wide to the point I would most likely need two hands just to jerk him off. Darius's grip on my waist has me focusing back on him. He smiles reassuringly at me and it eases some of the tension inside me. I lift up and line him up with my opening but before I sink down onto his waiting cock, he holds me steady as he looks to Beck and says.

"Only I get to fuck her bare, not you, got it?" Beckett raises his brow in a condescending way as he flicks his gaze to the side drawer to reveal foil packets waiting. Now that he got his answer, I push his hands away and slowly lower myself onto his glorious cock, I've only got half of him in me and already my pussy is clamping down on his shaft. I don't get to draw this out, he thrusts the rest of the way inside me, causing me to scream out in the best type of way. Beckett uses that moment to his advantage. He shoves his cock in my open mouth. I don't have a gag reflex but I do have a fucking jaw that cannot dislocate to accommodate his size. He stands on the bed with his hand fisted in my hair, fucking my face while I try to find my rhythm so I can fuck Darius.

"Fuck, Leah, swirl your tongue just like that." Tired of him dictating the way I suck his dick, I take over. I continue to rock my hips and bounce on Darius's cock as I grip the base of Beckett's and stroke as I bob my head up and down loving the moans that tear from his throat.

"Told you she could suck dick like a pro," Darius smugly says. To shut him and his smugness up I lift up and drop down hard twice. "Fuck, yeah, baby, like that." I follow his orders and keep doing that until Beckett yanks his cock from my mouth. Spit drips down my chin, I reach up to brush it away but Beck drops to his knees and shocks the fuck out of me when he pulls me to him and kisses the breath out of me, when he pulls back I'm a panting mess. I can feel an orgasm cresting and try to latch onto it, needing to come all over Darius's cock and marking him as mine.

"Don't come!" The command in Beckett's tone has me stopping, I watch as he grabs a foil packet from the drawer, making quick work of tearing it open with his teeth and sliding the condom on. He jumps back on the bed but this time he moves so that he is behind me. Darius's eyes blaze with a look I can't decipher. I bend down and place a chaste kiss to his lips and say.

"All you have to do is say stop and everything stops." His eyes search mine for a beat before he shakes his head.

"This is the one and only time, cross it off your bucket list and burn the fucker." My heart soars at the fact he remembers my list. He smashes his lips against mine in a kiss of ownership. I tear away from him when I feel liquid sliding down the crack of my ass, I peer over my shoulder to see Beck squirting some KY on me and his cock. Darius wraps his arms around me keeping me plastered to his chest, without permission my pussy flutters drawing a satisfied smirk from the arrogant bastard whose cock is currently buried deep inside it.

"Try not to tense and try not to come." I frown at Beckett's words.

"Why can't I come?" I ask.

"You can but only when I'm inside you. If you come before, your body's natural reaction is to repel me from you. Darius is going to work you up and keep you focused on him while I slip in." The excitement of knowing I'm about to have two cocks inside me at the same time has me grinding my pussy down on Darius. He kisses me as I continue to ride him. I feel Beck circling my ass and slowly pushing using his finger to push the lube inside me. I moan into Darius's mouth. He and I have done anal a few times previously—it wasn't a favorite of mine but I also didn't hate it. When Beck uses his finger to fuck my ass and stretch me open a sheen of sweat begins to coat my body. "That's it, just keep doing that," he says as he pulls his finger free. I feel him lining the head of his cock up with my ass, not warning me when he pushes the tip inside.

"Fuck!" I cry out as I break the kiss. Beck snakes his arm around my front grips my throat and pulls my back flush against his chest before leaning around and kissing me. He uses my moment of surprise to sink deeper inside me, I moan into his mouth. Darius reaches up and cups my heavy boobs, brushing his thumbs over my hardened nipples. I slowly begin to rock into Beck only to feel Darius shift inside my pussy but in the best fucking way.

"Fuck you feel so tight!" Darius growls. I pull away from Beck to lean down on Darius to give him better access into my ass. Beck grips my ass cheeks and pushes them apart, he rocks back and forward easing into me as moans continue to tumble from me. It feels like torture—Darius is hard and ready in my greedy cunt while Beck is taking his sweet ass time pushing into me. The need to come is overwhelming which is why I shout.

"Just fucking do it!" He obeys my order and fuck me seven ways sideways. The pain that accompanies the feeling of pleasure is only drowned out when Darius thrusts his hips into me continuously as if knowing an orgasm is the only way to get me over the urge to scream at Beck to get the fuck out of me. He is too big. The harder Darius fucks me the more the urge to get Beck to match his pace wars inside me. "Beckett, fuck me," I moan as I lay my hands flat on Darius's chest and attempt to hold on. If you have ever had two men inside you at the same time, you will know that when the orgasm crashes into you it is like nothing you have ever experienced before. It feels like your body is being ripped apart and sewed back together while having your pussy eaten exactly like you dreamed of. "Fuck yes, fuck me like that," I scream as I ride out my orgasm and come all over Darius's cock.

I slump forward onto Darius's chest, spent and wrung out in the best possible way. Beck pulls out of me and suddenly I feel empty. That feeling doesn't last long when his hands grip my waist and I'm lifted off of Darius, and spun around. I wrap my legs around his waist and rest my hands on the tops of his shoulders staring at him in surprise. Beck lines his cock up with my opening and slowly pushes inside me, my gaze holds his the entire time. Something about looking him in the eye as his cock eases inside my pussy is erotic.

"Fuck, you feel so good," he grits out before slamming his lips to mine. His grip on my ass tightens as his pace begins to quicken. I moan, loving the feeling of him inside me, stretching me. I gasp and break the kiss to look over my shoulder when I feel Darius at my back. He places a kiss to my cheek as he runs his hand down my back and slaps my ass causing me to shriek in surprise.

"My turn, baby," he says. Beckett moves his hands to my waist as Darius parts my cheeks and pushes the head of his cock inside my ass. Heat begins to spread throughout my body, he's pushing inside at the same time Beck lazily thrusts inside me. I lean back against Darius, the move allows me to sink onto his cock and gives Beckett better access to pound into my greedy pussy. Like the both of them are mind readers they give me exactly what I want. Beckett's thrusts begin to grow harder, surer while Darius slips all the way inside me. Darius grips my thighs and pulls them open so I'm practically doing the splits in the air. I cry out, at this angle the both of them feel so fucking deep and fuck me, it feels amazing!

"Jesus, hold her like that," Beck demands, a fine sheen of sweat dots his forehead. "Fuck yes, I'm gonna come like this."

I shake my head. "No. I want the both of you to come at the same time." The pair of them eye each other over my shoulder for a second before they come to some kind of agreement and start pounding into both my holes. It takes a solid minute before I'm screaming at them not to fucking stop, I feel my orgasm cresting ready to rip through me like a welcome tidal wave.

"Get there, D, I'm about to come," Beckett growls. Darius's grip on my thighs turns punishing, his fingerprints will be marked into my flesh for the next few days.

"Fuck!" Darius shouts from behind me as he comes. I scream his name at the top of my lungs as I shatter on their cocks. Beck roars out his own release. Tonight has been the most euphoric night of my life and the best sex I have ever had. I gave up on the idea of ever crossing this off my bucket list because there was only one person I wanted to experience it with. Thanks to a twist of fate and my brother being out of town, my beautiful dream became a reality. The only sounds that can be heard are our heavy breaths. Beck's green eyes bore into me and I frown when he shoots me a grateful smile.

"Swear to God, if you say thank you, I'll head butt you," I say. Beck and Darius both laugh, I don't because I am 100% serious. Beck shakes his head and smiles kindly at me. Something about the way he is looking at me tells me that what just happened between us wasn't just for my benefit.

"I'm gonna pull out, you ready?" I nod as Beck slowly eases out of me, then grips my waist and helps me to my feet. An involuntary shudder rolls through me when I feel the cum dripping out of my ass.

"Come on, let's get you in the shower." I nod and let Darius lead me to the bathroom. He flicks the shower on and holds his hand under the running water. When the water reaches the temperature he likes he steps back and ushers me into the stall. I turn to close the glass door but pause when I see him stepping in behind me. I shoot him a questioning look, he just shrugs and says, "There's a drought somewhere so we should conserve water and all that shit."

"A drought, really?" I laugh as I turn around and step under the spray, keen to wash off the cum currently leaking out of my ass. It's an odd feeling having something leak from your ass, no matter how much I try to clench it continues to leak out of me.

"Turn around." I do as he says and my heart melts when I see him holding my loofah. He proceeds to wash me thoroughly, making sure there is no surface of my body left unwashed. When he finally deems me clean, I snatch the loofah from him and return the favor, except unlike him when I drop to my knees to wash his legs, I have ulterior motives. I drop the loofah and grip the base of his cock, he's already growing hard. I peer up at him through my lashes and love the way his eyes darken as I slowly suck him into my mouth. I relish in the sounds he makes as I pleasure him. There is no greater feeling in the world then knowing that I may be on my knees, but I am the one who holds all the power.

CHAPTER NINETEEN

Darius

Her mouth feels like heaven.

I stretch my arms out wide to stabilize myself, then widen my stance to give her better access to my dick. She uses her hand to pump the base as she sucks the head swirling her tongue around the tip, then a low moan from her sends vibrations straight to my balls. As good as her mouth feels wrapped around me, I need to be inside her. I need to wash away Beck's touch by fucking her again and coming inside her tight cunt. I grip her hair and yank her head back, a small hiss escapes her mouth as she darts her stunned gaze to me.

"Get up," I growl, using my hold on her hair to help her to her feet. "Did you like Beck fucking your pussy?" Confusion colors her features. I slip my free hand between us and cup her sex. The confused look on her face vanishes and is instantly replaced by one of desire.

"Yes." I narrow my eyes as I push two fingers inside her, her mouth drops open to form a perfect O. I lean down and lick her bottom lip before sucking it into my mouth. I release her lip when a small whimper breaks free. She pushes down onto my fingers making me smirk.

"You just had two cocks inside you and yet your cunt is still hungry for more?"

"No. I'm just hungry for more of *you*." Her words shouldn't have my ego bolstering but they do. I yank her forward and mold my mouth to hers. I release my hold on her hair as I lift her, then back her up against the tiled wall. She arches forward to try escape the coldness of the tiles but I'm not allowing it, I use my weight to push her flat as I slowly lower her onto my shaft.

"This," I growl as I thrust inside her drawing a loud cry from her lips. "Is." Thrust. "Mine." I repeat those three words to her over and over again until we are both screaming the other's name like it's a Hail Mary play in the last quarter.

I wake to the sound of my alarm blaring. I reach out and grip my phone to snooze it. I sit up straight when I realize it's not the alarm but Corvin calling me. I slip out from beside Leah, careful not to wake her as I grab some shorts and leave the room, closing the door quietly. The call ends and starts again, I answer it on the second ring as I hold the phone between my shoulder and cheek while I pull on my shorts.

"What up?" I say.

"Dude I have been calling you for ages!" I roll my eyes and make my way downstairs as I answer him.

"You rang me once, don't be dramatic."

"Whatever, asshole," he says. I hear a door close and then some rustling before he speaks again. "Did you know Coach is ordering drug tests for the team?" I frown as I enter the kitchen, not sure why this news warrants a call at five in the fucking morning.

"So? Why do you care? It's not like any of us use drugs." When a sigh escapes him I tense. "Right?" His silence stretches and I curse under my breath as Beck walks into the kitchen shooting me a worried look. "Hold on Beck's here, I'm gonna put you on speaker." I put him on speaker and place the phone on the counter and I gather what I need for a protein shake.

"What's going on?" Beck asks as he begins to make his own shake.

"Coach wants us to take weekly drug tests. Apparently, someone made a complaint and said that CHU players are doping up on roids," Corvin grits out, Beck and I share a look of concern before I ask.

"Why are you acting so cagey, Corvin. What the fuck is going on?" A tired sigh comes through the phone and I brace myself for the worst.

"Dude, Kyle, Lance, Rick and Spencer have been kicked from the team already." My eyes shoot wide at that bit of news. "They swore black and blue that they never touched any drugs at the party they went to but the test doesn't lie." The anger in Corvin's voice matches how I'm feeling.

"Kyle and Spencer wouldn't risk their scholarships," Beck adds.

"I know. Something isn't right and given the test was administered here and not at school makes me think it's one of the other teams setting us up." At least six other colleges are at the camp Corv and the others are at which means, Gary and his team will be there and I'd put money on the fact it was that son of bitch that set up our guys.

"We need to get on top of this. We can't afford a scandal right now," I say.

"I know, why do you think I'm calling, dumbass?"

"Let me call Troy and see if there is any way we can push the merge up to next week. If we are all thinking it's the same person targeting our team then we need to be smart about it. Gary has the money to get people to do his bidding. Parties are out until after the merger and the season." Beck is right, we need to keep our heads on straight.

"Yeah, okay. I'll tell Saint and Crue but they won't like being on house arrest."

"I don't care, Corvin, we can't risk it. If you, Saint and Crue want to go pro then the three of you need to suck it up until we find out who the fuck is doing this," I growl.

"Yeah, okay. You and Beck call Troy and see if we can bring the merger forward. If we get that done, then we should be okay to take our time and figure this shit out." Beck and I agree before ending the call. The silence stretches between us and begins to grow uncomfortable, so I decide to leave him and hit the makeshift gym in the basement to get in a workout.

Ten minutes go by before the door opens and Beck walks in as I'm lifting weights. He goes for the treadmill to warm up. The only sound that can be heard is the music coming from the Bluetooth speaker. The both of us continue to work out in silence until it begins to get on my nerves that we have tension between us.

I know last night was a lot but, coupled with the news from Corvin, we can't afford to be divided right now when we have some fucker gunning for us. Unlike the other three, Beck and I know we don't have the skill set to go pro. We love the game and would kill to go pro but that isn't in the cards for us. We decided a long time ago that Beck and I would run the company and manage everything while the three of them worked their asses off to get drafted and play in the NFL. Saint needs this, if he doesn't get drafted his father has ordered him to take over his tech company, the company Saint hates.

"Are we good?" I place the dumbbell on the mat and turn to see Beck leaning against the treadmill with a towel draped around his neck. The uncertainty in his eyes vanishes the moment I shoot him a smile.

"Yeah, bro, we're always going to be good." The tension in his shoulders eases a bit.

"So, you gonna be good with me and Leah living under the same roof?" The smile vanishes from my face in an instant as old feelings resurface. I slam my eyes closed and try to block them out but it's fucking hard! "What happened, D?" I cover my face with my hands debating if I should tell him or not. "Darius, whatever happened between the two of you has been eating at you for years. I'm not prying or trying to be nosey, I am just genuinely worried about you."

The words spew out of me before I can stop them. "I told her not to go to the party after we won the final in high school as she wanted me to tell Corvin about us. I was going to, that night." I feel him drop down onto the weight bench beside me. I drop my hands and rest my forearms on the tops of my thighs as I hunch forward. "I knew she was serious this time when she said I either tell him or we're done. I weighed up the options and I fucking love Corvin but the truth is…"

"You love his sister more," Beck adds. A whoosh of air escapes me and I nod. "So what happened?"

"We got into a fight when I told her to stay home and that I would tell him at the party. She didn't listen. When I got to the party, Jeff told me Gary was there and upstairs with Corvin's sister. I raced up the stairs and what I saw… broke me man. She was naked and crashed on the bed while Gary was getting dressed. The bastard smiled and winked at me as he shouldered past. I stood there for like five minutes just staring at her naked ass until I heard Corvin yelling out for shots downstairs, I closed the door and left her there." Bitterness coats each of my words. I fucking hate Gary Hayes because that son of bitch knew exactly who Leah was to me and threatened to out me to Corv if I didn't shave points on the game. That motherfucker got his ass beat on the field and as payback, he slept with my girl and ruined the only good thing I had in my life aside from the guys.

"Jesus!" Beck says on an exhale. "I had no idea. I mean I knew something bad happened because you went from over protective to just... not giving a fuck where she was concerned."

"Yeah," I say in a dejected tone.

"Fuck and she went to DCU with him!"

"She sure fucking did, brother," I grit out. "Corv and I went home one year for Thanksgiving and guess who she brought to fucking dinner?" Beck's eyes widen as he shakes his head trying to deny my claim.

"No way."

"Yes, fucking way. I had to sit across the table from the motherfucker that fucked my girl and play nice because of Corvin and his parents. Want to know the worst fucking part?" I don't give him a chance to answer. "Leah acted like nothing happened and kept shooting me hurt looks like I was in the fucking wrong! I was about to lose my best friend that night by telling him I was in love with his sister. Thank God I found her first or else I would have lost Corv for nothing."

"Fuck. I had no idea man. I'm really fucking sorry that happened. I really didn't think Leah was like that."

"Yeah. Neither did I." I can hear the hurt that laces my own voice.

CHAPTER TWENTY

Leah

I wake with the biggest smile on my face. I reach out for Darius and frown when I can't find him next to me. I blink my eyes open only to find the space next to me vacant. I climb out of bed and grab one of his shirts from the floor and pull it on as I check the bathroom for him. Finding the space empty, I quickly relieve myself and brush my teeth before going in search of him. Before I can exit the room my phone rings and cringe at the ringtone. I rush into my room and grab it off my dresser and answer the dreadful call.

"What?" I snap.

"Good work, little mouse, four players down." I slam my eyes closed as guilt eats away at me.

"What the hell do you want?" I grit out. He is the last person I want to be hearing from first thing in the morning. I check the time on my phone and stifle a groan when I see it's only six-thirty in the freaking morning.

"The four players that are out aren't the ones I told you to take out! Fix this fucking shit now or–"

"Or what? You're gonna share the video? What proof do I have that you will even hand it over?"

His dark laughter fills the phone. "You don't. Now be a

good bitch and do as you're told, the game is in three weeks and they better not take the fucking field." He ends the call. I growl as I toss the fucking phone onto my bed and storm out of my room. I head downstairs in search of Darius only to find the space empty. I frown but then I hear the music playing and follow the sound to the basement, but at the sound of voices, I pause.

"Jesus!" Beck sound appalled. "I had no idea, I mean I knew something bad happened because you went from over protective to just... not giving a fuck where she was concerned."

"Yeah." Darius sounds so sad and it breaks my heart. I'm about to make my presence known until Beck speaks again.

"Fuck and she went to DCU with him!" They're talking about me!

"She sure fucking did brother. Corv and I went home one year for Thanksgiving and guess who she brought to fucking dinner?" Shame washes over me knowing which Thanksgiving he is talking about.

"No way."

"Yes, fucking way, I had to sit across the table from the motherfucker that fucked my girl and play nice because of Corvin and his parents. Want to know the worst fucking part?" Tears prick the backs of my eyes knowing how that must have looked to him. "Leah acted like nothing happened and kept shooting me hurt looks like I was in the fucking wrong! I was about to lose my best friend that night by telling him I was in love with his sister. Thank God I found her first or else I would have lost Corv for nothing." He thinks he knows what he saw but he has no fucking idea and that has my stomach churning.

"Fuck. I had no idea man. I'm really fucking sorry that happened. I really didn't think Leah was like that."

"Yeah. Neither did I." I slam my eyes closed and lean my head back against the wall as the first tear falls. I hate that he thinks of me like this but if I tell him, he will never look at me the same again! "I fucking loved her man. She was the first person I ever let in and now I'm so fucked up because of it. I can't even look at another girl or kiss them while I fuck them because it hurts to know they aren't her. Fuck." The devastation in his voice is killing me! "She is the only girl I have ever kissed, how fucked is that?" He laughs but there's no humor to it. "Want to know something else that is so fucked up?" He doesn't give Beckett a chance to answer. "I still fucking love her and that is what fucks with my head daily!"

That's it, I can't listen to any more of this shit!

I round the corner with tears trailing down my cheeks, both their heads snapping up at the sound of my arrival. Darius looks devastatingly beautiful, even with the angry look on his face. I hate that I am the one who hurt him so badly. I will never forgive myself for that but I made the mistake of not coming clean when I found out months ago. If I'm going down I refuse to take any of these guys with me.

"Eavesdropping?" Darius snarls, his eyes shine with hatred and I can't blame him for that. Beck stands to leave to give us some privacy but I shoot him a look and shake my head. "Oh, you gonna fuck my best friend as well, Goldie?"

I look back to Darius and plead with my eyes that he can see I didn't hurt him purposely. I didn't mean for any of this to happen. "I'm sorry," I sob. He climbs to his feet and runs his gaze up and down my body in disgust, the way he looks at me is like I'm shit beneath his shoe and it kills me.

"I thought I could give you the four days, I really did," he says, shaking his head. "Seems I can't do it," is all he says before storming from the room and yanking my heart out of my chest again. Sobs tear from me, they steal the breath from my lungs as I crumple to the floor crying for the boy who was meant to be mine. I bury my face in my hands and cry, if I thought losing him the first time was bad, this time it feels like I won't survive. Strong arms wrap around me and lift me into his lap. I cling to Beck as I bury my face in his shirt and soak it with my tears.

"Why do I feel like there is more to this story and that you never cheated on him?" he quietly asks after my sobs finally subside enough for me to breathe a bit easier. I sniff and burrow into him, he rests his chin atop my head.

"There is more but I can't tell you," I whisper. I feel him exhale and know he is disappointed in the fact I won't just come clean.

"If you really love him like I think you do, you need to fix this, Leah, because Darius can't handle another person letting him down."

"What do you mean?" I ask.

"If he finds out I told you this he is going to kick my ass."

"I won't say anything, I swear," I rush out.

"His dad… he left and that fucked D up more than you will ever know." I knew about this, his dad skipped town or something when his mom got pregnant and Darius has no idea who he is. "His mom is a fucking junkie and will sell her body for her next hit. All he had was you, Corv and your parents, until Saint, Crue and me came along. Darius doesn't have anyone, only me, Saint, Crue and your brother. For him to have trusted you was a huge thing. He let you in, Leah, and he doesn't let anyone in."

"I don't understand," I say confused.

"Leah?" He pushes me back until we are staring each other in the eyes, his face is serious. "He has never let any of us in, only you. We all know what Darius wants us to know but none of us can read him or know what his next move is. I saw it years ago. You can read him and that's because he let you in. If whatever happened years ago isn't what he thinks it was, you need to tell him because I won't watch him fuck up his life again."

"Again?" I hedge, he takes a shuddering breath and nods.

"Darius was wild and angry when we first got here. None

of us knew why and he wouldn't let us help him. He threw himself into training. He trains harder than anyone on the team and applies himself to everything he does even when we started the comp... He is crazy smart and buries himself in work because he thinks hiding from his feelings will make them go away. You coming back brought everything he thought he had worked through back to the surface and it is scaring the hell out of him."

"It scares me too. I love him, Beck, and I hate that I hurt him but I don't have a choice," I defend, his eyes soften as he runs his knuckles along my cheek, not in a sexual way but in a comforting way.

"We all have a choice, Leah. You just need to decide if the choice you are making is benefiting you or not. Whatever you are hiding from and keeping from him is hurting him. Darius isn't the type of guy to play games. If you push him too far, he will snap and you will never get him back. Make your choice, babe, but make sure it's one you can live with." I smile sadly up at him.

"How did you get so wise about relationship advice?" I ask teasingly, not expecting him to answer.

"I fucked up a long time ago with someone who meant everything to me, so I can relate to how Darius is feeling."

After leaving Beck in the basement, I decided it was best for me to move out. Cody and Katie said they would make room for me in their dorm room. I took the offer and packed my shit. As soon as Beck and Darius left to hit the gym at school, I texted Cody. She drove over and helped me load my things and brought me back to their dorm. I have a futon on the floor and the room is jam packed with all our things but it beats living next door to Darius. I just need some space from him, need to think about what I'm going to do next.

I know if I go through with this plan, I will definitely lose him. Me telling him about what happened is one thing but him seeing it is another. I feel sick every time I think about it.

"Want to tell us why *Da-Leah* is a no go anymore?" Katie's softly asked question pulls me from my inner thoughts. I sigh and sit cross legged on my futon as each of them lays on their beds on their stomachs facing me, waiting for an answer.

"Everything was great until it wasn't," I answer.

"Well what happened yesterday after you took off?" Cody asks. I fill them in on how Darius and Beck found me but I don't share details about how the rest of our night went. What happened between the three of us is private and no one else's business. "So, if everything was good, why are you here? I mean we're glad to have you here but I'm just trying to piece it together."

"My past came back to bite me in the ass and Darius can't let it go, and I can't explain it to him."

"Why not?" Katie's question is innocent but if she knew the truth she would understand that I can't.

"Because I can't. I wish more than anything I could give him what he wants but I'm too much of a coward." I wrap my arms around my middle and drop my chin to my chest ashamed and disgusted in myself for the choices I have made.

CHAPTER TWENTY-ONE

Darius

"What up, fuckers?" Saint shouts as he, Crue and Corv burst through the front door. I smile wide as each of them waltz into the living room and give me a hug hello. Beck walks in and greets each of the guys, the four of them drop down onto the couches. They looked fucking wrecked.

"Where's Leah?" Corvin asks. Beck and I share a quick look before I answer.

"She moved out." When we got home yesterday, Beck went to check on her and found her room empty. I spent the rest of the night in the gym working out my anger that she just left. In hindsight it was a good thing because with her not being here it's going to be a lot easier to keep my dick out of her.

"What the fuck do you mean?" Corv growls as he shifts forward in his seat pinning me with a look. I throw my hands up in the air and roll my eyes frustrated.

"What the fuck are you looking at me like that for? I didn't do shit." I'm lying through my teeth but I don't care.

"I'm not blaming you for shit. I'm asking *you* why she left and didn't tell me?"

"I don't know, she's your sister so maybe call the impulsive little shit and find out," I grit out through clenched teeth.

"Someone must be on their bitchy time of the month," Crue jokes, earning a glare from me. "Oh, calm down, we just got back and don't even get a day off tomorrow before we have to train. So, how about we order in some pizza and go over this merger and read the fine print because we all know that fucker will try and stiff us in the fine print." Each of us voices our agreement as we head off to shower and leave Crue to order the pizza. I make quick work of showering, step out and wrap a towel around my waist before going to my room. I freeze when I see Corvin sitting on the end of my bed with a black thong dangling from his finger, shit!

He wiggles his brows suggestively at me as he says, "Been busy plowing through pussy while I was away. Anyone I know?" I swallow the retort that is on the tip of my tongue as I turn and head for my dresser as I answer him.

"I think you've seen her around." If only he knew that the thong currently dangling from his finger belonged to his sister.

"Just wanted to check in and see if Leah said anything to you or Beck about why she transferred?" I drop my towel and laugh when Corvin begins to curse me out for having my ass on display.

"Nah, man," I say as I pull on a pair of sweats and turn to face him. His face falls and I hate that I keep lying to him but it's just the way it has to be.

"Yeah, okay. Come on, we need to sort out this merger before we get fucked." I nod and follow after him. Crue, Saint and Beck are sitting in the living room with boxes of Pizzas set out on the coffee table. Corv and I snag a box each. As we drop into the vacant two-seater, Beck hands out a folder to each of us.

"These have the contracts in them. I spoke with Troy and we are set on our end. Sullivan Global management is willing to stay and keep things running, as well as show us each the day to day operations. I'm happy to do that once we finish school, are you all okay with that?" The four of us agree, Beck will be the perfect man for the job. He's a fast learner and takes pride in everything he does. "I think we make Darius the face of the company when the merger is complete."

"No!" I snap.

"You are the one who will be based out of the office in the city. You will fill the position as CFO until I can grasp the day-to-day shit with the hotels and resorts." We may own the stock market and dominate in that field, but acquiring Sullivan Global means we are branching out into foreign waters. They don't just fuck with the stock market, they also own hotel chains worldwide and resorts in Alaska, Hawaii, Australia, Japan and New Zealand. "It was your idea to bring them down and that shit you leaked to the papers is the only reason we are in the position to afford to buy them out. We need this, D." I scrub a hand down my face. If this is the sacrifice I need to make for my brothers, then so be it.

"Fine, but any board meetings the four of you have to sit in on them because I'm not making decisions on my own." I look to each of them letting know how serious I am about this point. Honestly, I'm nervous as fuck to be doing this on my own. I've always had them with me, so the thought of us all parting ways when school is over has me feeling scared. Crue, Saint and Corv have their football shit lined up, but Beck will head off to Alaska to learn the ropes and then I'll be here on my own.

"Deal, if we can't be there in person we'll be on video," Saint suggests and I agree.

"Man, if someone asked me what I would be doing at twenty I would never think this would be it." I grunt my agreement, Corv is right.

"We built this whole company from the ground up at sixteen and now look at us. We are about to be Forbes richest." We all laugh at Crue. we won't be the richest but we will live without worry for the rest of our lives.

"I don't think I have ever said it before, but thank you guys." The serious tone of Saint's voice has me sitting straighter. "You all knew that I hated the thought of ever running my dad's company and I fucking hate him, but I didn't have a way out until now. So, thank you all for helping me." Crue wraps an arm around his shoulders and gives him a side hug. Saint's dad is a piece of shit. He may have bought us this house but it wasn't from the kindness of his heart. If Saint doesn't take over for his father, he has to pay him back every cent for his tuition, living costs and this house. He thinks Saint doesn't have his own money, but thanks to this merger, Saint can buy his freedom and in turn take his fucking father down.

"We all helped each other," I say. "Without all of you I would have been under a bridge somewhere so the feeling is mutual, brother." Corvin slaps me on the shoulder and pins me with a look that says over his dead body that would have happened.

"Okay, we officially settle on SG next Tuesday and once that is final and underway, we focus on taking down Lexington Corp." The four of us nod our agreement. "Once we finally finish this, what next?" Beck's question has stumped me. I have no idea how to answer that. For years all we have focused on is this end goal and nothing else. What do I want to do with my life? A picture flashes through my mind of a house on the beach and a gorgeous blonde on a surfboard, but I shake that away.

"I plan to play in the NFL for as long as I can then retire, buy a yacht and drown in pussy for the rest of my days." We all groan and mutter about Saint being a dick.

"Once I hang my boots up for the last time, I'm gonna travel and see the fucking world." I could really see Crue being a tourist.

"Mine starts now." I furrow my brow at Corv. "When this is done, I'm coming out to my parents and buying them a house in the mountains like they have always wanted and never let them work again. I'll get Leah set up somewhere before I leave and hire guards so no fucker can get near my baby sister. Best part is, with us being the majority shareholders in the school, Leah will never have to pay for her schooling." I turn away from him, not able to look at him knowing I'm the one who took his sister's innocence. We spend the rest of the night talking shit and allowing ourselves to finally breathe a bit easier knowing that this is all going to work out. We fucking did it. Excitement thrums through me at the thought of seeing the looks on their faces when they find out it was me that ruined their lives and they had no fucking idea. He thought he fucked me over. That dumb fuck was playing a quick game while I was playing the long game from the start. Touchdown, motherfucker, I'm coming for you.

CHAPTER TWENTY-TWO

Leah

The week goes by in a blur, I've managed to avoid my brother and only speak to him on the phone, but I know it won't last. I've managed to avoid all five of them. I hate hearing how they are worshiped and looked up to as kings. It fucking grates on my nerves more when I have practice every day and have to hear Chelsea talk about how her and Darius are meant to be. Nikki thinks Beck is going to whisk her away and treat her like the queen she thinks she is. Both these bitches are bat shit crazy. We've run the same counts six times because Donald can't get the steps and it is grating on my nerves. I just want to get the hell out of here!

"Okay, listen up." Thankful for the reprieve I place my hands on my knees and take some deep breaths as we wait for coach to speak. "I have some bad news, we won't be dancing at the championship." Shouts and boos erupt from around me. "Quiet!" Coach yells, then blows her whistle. "I know you are all pissed off but there isn't a thing we can do. The school board tried but the other schools vetoed the idea and said no." I deflate, this is like a kick in the gut. This was our one chance to showcase our skills and show everyone we are more than some dance team that teaches girls how to shake their assess.

"Why the hell are we training so hard then?" Donald calls out, a devilish smirk graces coach's face.

"I said the school said no, I never said I agreed." Gasps ring out. "I mean I could never condone you all going against the school as a faculty member but I mean, if I taught you a kick ass routine and you all happen to rush onto the field at halftime and do said dance, who am I to stop you?" Everyone screams in excitement. Cody, Katie and I all scream and do an awkward three way hug. This is exactly the type of news I needed. After everything with Darius, I really needed a pick me up!

"Seriously, pineapple on a pizza?" I glare across the table at Garrett, who raises his hands in surrender. The girls and I ran into him after practice. We didn't tell him why we were happy, just that we got good news, so he insisted on taking us for pizza to celebrate. After the workout we just did, who are we to turn down free carbs?

"What's wrong with it?" I say around a mouthful of food, causing him to laugh and a blush to raise to my cheeks.

"What's right with it? It doesn't belong on a pizza, it shouldn't even be classed as a topping!" Cody and Katie both chime in with their agreement, which just earns them an eye roll from me.

"It's great, try it," I say as I pick up another slice and hold it out to him. His face scrunches in disgust, making me laugh. The girls join in when he recoils back into his seat as I lean over the table and hold it practically in front of his face.

"Well, what do we have here?" The smile vanishes from my face. At the sound of his voice, all the muscles in my body go rigid. Garrett sits up straighter as I slowly lower back into my seat and drop the pizza on my plate, keeping my gaze focused on it. I can feel Katie and Cody staring at me but I can't move, what the hell is he doing here? "Don't get all shy on me, little mouse, I drove all the way here just to see you." When his meaty hand lands on my shoulder I flinch away. At the sound of Garrett's chair scraping back, I snap my gaze to him and watch him stand up.

Shit!

"What the fuck are you doing here, Hayes?" I frown confused as to how he knows Gary but then it hits me, he's on the same team as the guys, so of course he would know him.

"Just came to visit an old friend," he says as he grips my shoulder again. This time he squeezes it so hard a whimper escapes me.

"Get your fucking hands off her now!" Garrett snarls. I peek over my shoulder to see Gary didn't come alone. There are at least six guys with him and they look like they are ready to throw down.

"Or what? You think you can take us, on your own?" he mocks. Garrett darts his gaze to me and I plead with my eyes not to do anything stupid.

"He won't, but I fucking will." It's been five days since I have heard his voice and it's a welcome balm to my tattered nerves. Gary's grip on my shoulder tightens the moment he feels me relax, a whimper escapes again. I hear him move toward us and tense in preparation for what is to come. He comes to a stop in front of us. I look up and find his brown eyes laser focused on Gary's hand that is gripping my shoulder in a punishing hold. He snaps his hand out, grips Gary's wrist and shoves him back a step. Gary rights himself quickly and gets in Darius's face. D has a few inches on Gary and you can tell from his posture that he hates it.

"You think you stand a chance alone? There are seven of us, you piece of shit!" Gary spits right in Darius's face.

Instead of backing down or rethinking his move, Darius smiles cockily.

"Who said anything about him being alone?" I look past the two guys to see Saint, Corvin, Crue and Beckett marching toward us like gods with fury written over each of their faces. They come to a stop behind Darius, the bond each of these guys shares is awe inspiring. I can kind of see why everyone worships them. "Now, unless you want us to leave tread marks all over you and your band of cheerleaders' faces, I suggest you get the fuck out of our town." I've never heard Crue sound... so serious or aggressive before.

"Take the warning and fuck off," Darius says in a tone so low and deadly it sends a shudder through me. Gary pulls back, smiles and brushes the nonexistent wrinkles from Darius's shoulders then turns to me. The look in his soulless blue eyes has my breath hitching. He tilts his head forward causing his brown hair to flop onto his forehead. The guy thinks he can pull off the *Jax Teller* hairstyle but he really can't. His teeth are crooked and the fact he has a tongue ring with a dice on it makes me ill.

"Don't worry, mouse, I'll be seeing you again real, *real* soon." I say nothing as he and his band of misfits push their way through Corvin and the others. The moment the restaurant door closes, I sag into my seat, ecstatic that my nightmare is gone.

My reprieve is short lived.

"What the fuck was that, Goldie?" I slowly lift my gaze to Darius's and a whirl of emotions war in his eyes—anger, confusion, hatred but the worst of all it's when I see betrayal that it burns me.

"I don't know," I say as I stand, grab my jacket and bag. The girls follow my lead and quickly gather their things, while Garrett drops some bills on the tables. I try to move past Darius and the others but they form a wall, a hulking fucking wall full of glares and accusations. "Excuse me," I grit out.

"Answer him, Leah. What the fuck was Gary doing here?" Corvin sounds pissed and I can't blame him, I decide to go with the truth.

"I have no idea, we came here to celebrate after practice and then he just showed up." I hold my brother's gaze so he can see the truth in my eyes. "I swear, Corv, we were just hanging out and then he... ruined it." I whisper the last part. Corvin reaches out and places his hands on the top of my shoulders. I hiss and flinch away. Before I can take a full step back, Darius is in front of me ripping the sleeve of my shirt down to expose my shoulder, which I know will already be bruising. His eyes darken at the sight of it, he grips the back of my neck and pulls me into him until his forehead rests against mine.

"You are going to tell me everything, but right now, I have a quarterback's arm to break." He releases me and races from the restaurant with the other four following him. I take a second to gather myself before I'm following after them. I break through the door in time to see Gary and his friends peeling out of the car park in their cars, hollering out the window. "Fucking pussy ass bitches!" Darius roars as he watches their cars driveaway. When he turns back to face us, his gaze finds mine immediately. "Say goodbye to your friends, your ass is coming with us!" My mouth unhinges. I look to Corvin expecting him to stop him but the bastard just crosses his arms over his chest and quirks a brow at me, daring me to defy king broody beside him.

"I can take you back." I turn my head to the side to see Garrett, standing there with his hands in his jeans pockets. I smile kindly, ready to accept his offer but the king asshole cuts me off.

"Accept his offer, Goldie, and see what happens." I cut a glare to Darius, narrowing my eyes in warning as I grit out,

"You gonna tell my brother..." his eyes shoot wide, "on me?" I smirk when his face becomes a picture of annoyance. "Just so we are clear, I don't live with you lot anymore and newsflash, assholes, I'm eighteen!" I shout. The smirk that crosses Darius's face has the triumphant feeling inside me dwindling rapidly.

"Either Corvin throws you over his shoulder and puts your ass in the car or I do. Those are your only choices!" I look to the girls and shoot them a look that has them grinning like fools before turning to Garrett who just looks pissed off.

"Thanks for tonight," I say.

"Don't even think about–"

I cut Darius off before he can finish his threat. "Run!"

CHAPTER TWENTY-THREE

Darius

She screams she's eighteen and then runs off like a fucking child!

"Beck, Corv, get the cars, You two with me," I bark out as I race after the pain in my ass. Crue and Saint are right with me as we chase down the girls. I see them dart across the road heading for the park. It's fucking dark out and these idiots are running into a park surrounded by woodlands? Fucking morons. We race across the road. Gaining on them, the moment we hit the grass of the park, Leah looks over her shoulder and shouts.

"Split up!" I growl. She is going to pay for this. Her friends do as she ordered and break away in separate directions.

"Saint get Cody. Crue get Katie. I got the little shit," I snarl as I sprint after her. I'm only a couple steps behind her when I break through the brush. She chances another look over her shoulder and squeals out a laugh, then darts around a tree and I lose sight of her for a couple seconds. I round the same tree and come to a halt when I don't see her anywhere.

"Boo." I snap my gaze to the side where she leans against

the tree, huffing. I crowd her space and place my arms on either side of her head, caging her in. Our breaths are coming in rapid pants thanks to her impromptu race. The smile that is plastered on her face pisses me off.

"You think this is funny?" I snap.

"Yeah, I do actually." Her sarcastic reply grates on my already frayed nerves. "You act all big and tough, and pretend to hate me but look where you are, Darius. You had a choice to chase three girls and from what I heard back there you didn't even have to think about which one you were gunning for!" She steps into me so our chests brush against each other, then grips the sides of my shirt keeping me anchored in place as she slowly cranes her neck back to meet my gaze. "You either want me or you let me fucking go because I can't keep playing this game with you."

"Game?" I snarl as I yank free of her hold, putting a couple feet of space between us. "You think this is a fucking game?" I roar. She shrinks back into the tree but my temper is too far gone to be controlled. "None of this was ever a fucking game to me. This is my life you are destroying just by being near me! I fucking hate you, Leah." She flinches and drops her gaze to her shoes as her shoulders hunch forward. "I'll never fucking forgive you for what you did to me, I can't," I grit out before storming away from her. I break the tree line to find Beck standing there with a pitying look on his face. Before I can say anything, he holds out the keys to his car and flicks his head toward where it is parked at the curb.

"Saint and Crue have the girls in there, drop them at their dorm and grab her a bag. I'll get her and bring her back with me and Corvin." I nod my thanks and begin to move away but his words have me halting. "She's right, though. You either want her or you don't, you need to decide." The only response he gets is a grunt before I'm storming off toward his car.

I made Cody pack her bag and smacked Saint across the back of the head when he offered to pick out her panties. After leaving the girls, we headed straight home and have been sitting in the car for five minutes. I know we have to go in but I don't want to. Beckett's words keep replaying over and over in my mind. They may be true but it's fucking hard to let go of your first love. What makes the whole situation more fucked up is I can't even escape my first and only girlfriend because she is my best friend's little fucking sister!

"You know if we don't go in we'll never find out why Gary was here." Crue's attempt to get me out of the car works, my curiosity is peaked and I need answers. We storm through the door only to find Beck and Corv sitting in the living room, *alone*. At the sound of our entry Corvin slowly turns his head toward us and pins me with an angry fucking look that promises pain.

"Gary fucking Hayes doesn't walk off the field. That motherfucker goes out in a box!" I dart my gaze between Beck and Corvin utterly fucking confused.

"What happened?" I hedge. Corv jumps to his feet and flips the coffee table before storming up the stairs. When I hear his bedroom door slam shut, I look to Beck for answers. He shakes his head and stands.

"All I know is, he hurt her and Corvin won't tell me any more than that. Him showing up tonight wasn't because she wanted him there. You need to talk to her, Darius, because Corvin is out for blood." Beck turns and heads up the stairs to check on Corv I presume.

"Dude, what the fuck did we miss?" Saint mumbles as he brushes past me and heads for the kitchen. Crue pats me on the shoulder as he heads for the basement. I stand here stunned and fucking confused as hell as to what happened in the twenty minutes it took us to get here. I'm too angry to go to her, so instead, I drop her bag at the base of the stairs, grab two beers from the fridge and head out the back to kick it by the pool. I kick my shoes off and drop down onto the ledge of the pool not giving a fuck that my jeans are getting wet as I kick my legs back and forward into the water. I grab one of the beers and twist the cap off before downing half the bottle. I don't normally drink but the cluster fuck of events from the past few days has me needing it.

Just as I finish the last bottle of beer, I hear the door open behind me. Looking over my shoulder, I see Corv coming toward me with two beers in each hand. He hands me two before dropping down beside and placing his feet in the water. We sit here silently, sipping our beers and looking up at the night sky. The silence isn't tense or uncomfortable. Sometimes, it's actually nice to not be alone with your thoughts and have someone to just sit with you. I never knew what that was like growing up. I was banished to my room to fend for myself while my mom *worked*. Having an addict and a whore as a mother fucking sucked but her being useless led me to Corvin and his family, and for that reason only, I can't hate my childhood. I made a vow to myself the night I moved into the Williams' house, I would never allow myself to become like my mother and still to this day I have never touched a single illegal substance.

"He hurt her," Corvin's whispered words pull me from my inner thoughts, my temper has settled enough for me to talk now.

"What did she say?" I ask in an even tone.

He runs a hand through his hair in frustration. "It wasn't what she said, D, it was in her eyes. I could see the fear. She completely shut down when I asked her if he had ever hurt her at school. She went pale, started screaming that she was so sorry for being a fuck up and if she could change it she would, then ran upstairs to her room."

I mull over his words trying to make sense of what he is

saying. Tonight I saw that same look on her face when I walked through the door and saw his hand on her. At the sound of my voice I saw her relax almost like she was grateful that I was there to get him away from her. If that is the case and she is scared of him, what changed from them fucking to her being fearful of him?

"What do you want to do, Corv?" I ask.

"I want to bury the fucker six feet deep for ever hurting her. This is what I have always been scared of, her finding a guy and him being a piece of shit! Why couldn't she end up with one of you guys," he says before he begins to laugh. Meanwhile, I sit here frozen.

"Would that be a bad thing… if she did end up with one of us?" I keep my tone light, trying to act nonchalant when in truth, my heart is beating so fucking fast. He bumps me with his shoulder and snorts.

"Dude, I would fucking rip all of your dicks off if any of you touched my sister. I know what you fuckers get up to behind closed doors and that isn't happening where Leah is concerned." I force out a laugh for his benefit but inside my hope of him ever accepting me and Leah together fizzes out. "We have a couple weeks before the season starts and we play them, I want him carted off the fucking field and out for the whole season. I don't know exactly what he did to her but I know he did *do* something to her and he's going to fucking pay for that!" I grunt out my agreement.

Morning times in this house are fucking chaos. We all fight over the toaster and cereal boxes like pigs. Don't even get me started on what it's like when the five of us make protein shakes at the same time.

"You used all the fucking milk!" Crue shouts. Beck shrugs his shoulders as he scoops another mouthful of his breakfast into his mouth. "You asshole, now I have to have toast!" Crue is always a grumpy bitch first up in the morning.

"Dude, I'll buy you a bagel when we stop to get coffee." Crue beams at Saint.

"You do love me!" Crue sing songs.

"More than anything!" Saint replies in a fake British accent.

"Leah?" The four of us all turn toward the door to see Corv rushing toward his sister who looks like shit. She has dark circles under her eyes, her hair is piled on top of her head in a messy bun. She wears a loose fitting tee that she has knotted in the front and plain black yoga pants. "Are you okay?" She nods in answer to her brother's softly asked question. "Uh, want a lift to school?" Again she doesn't respond verbally, just shakes her head and tries to move around Corvin but he blocks her path. "Talk to me, Leah, what's going on?" he pleads.

"Nothing, I'm fine, everything is fine and dandy. Now can I go or I'll be late for practice." Stunned by her response, he nods and reluctantly steps out of her way, letting her walk right out the door without a fucking fight.

"Why the fuck did you let her leave?" I snap the second the front door clicks closed. Corvin spins around to face me looking utterly lost.

"What did you want me to do?" he growls angrily.

"Chain her ass to the bed if you had to!" I can hear the anger in my own voice. He eyes me warily for a second before asking,

"Since when do you care so much about *my* sister?" The accusation in his tone is clear. I should try to cover my ass but I'm tired of choosing between the Williams siblings. Like Beck said, I need to make a choice and I think I have. I stand, grab my bag off the floor, sling it over my shoulder and close the space between Corvin and me until we are standing an inch apart.

"I've always cared, more than you know or should I say more than you cared to see. I was the one who was worried about her while you were out dipping your dick in whatever had a hole. So don't fucking stand there and question my motives where *she* is concerned." I leave him standing there with a stunned look on his face as I chase after Leah.

CHAPTER TWENTY-FOUR

Leah

I don't get more than a few meters from the house before I hear someone running after me. I spin around ready to tell whoever it is to fuck off but clamp my mouth closed when I find it's Garrett.

"Morning, sunshine." I try to smile but from the look on his face I guess I fail. "Not such a good morning then, huh?" A whoosh of air escapes me as I shake my head.

"Not really," I answer honestly.

"How about I walk you to school and we can grab a coffee and chat?" I open my mouth to answer but clamp it closed when Darius appears out of thin air and answers for me.

"She's with me," is all he says. Garrett's eyes blaze with fury.

"She doesn't belong to you!" he snaps. Darius winks at him before shocking the hell out of me when cups my face and smashes his mouth to mine. The kiss isn't deep or anything like that, this kiss is for a purpose and that is to show Garrett that I'm Darius's. I want to fight him off and demand he never touch me but this is the first time he has ever kissed me publicly and in front of someone! He pulls back, smirks at me before wrapping an arm around my shoulders and hauling me away from a wide-eyed Garrett.

"I think he gets the hint now, don't you?" The gleeful sound of his voice snaps me out of my stupor. I pull away from him and quicken my pace to try to escape but of course he isn't having any of that and grips my bag yanking me back into his side.

"Leave me alone!" I hiss as I struggle to get away from him. He spins me around so I am facing him and cups my face.

"I can't," he says softly

"I thought you hated me?" I spit the words at him. He bends until we are eye level and I can see the seriousness in his eyes.

"I'm gonna tell you something before I let you run away to practice." I plaster a bored look on my face. "One, I am going to get to the bottom of why you freaked out on Corv last night." I struggle to keep my face blank when inside fear is threatening to cripple me, when he finds out the truth he is going to hate me. "Two, I do hate you." I suck a sharp intake of breath in as his words spear me right in the heart again. "I hate you because I can't fucking hate you. I keep thinking the more I say it might make it true." My mouth slackens in shock. "I hate that I can't hate you, Goldie. I fucking hate that you can still have me wrapped around your finger and I'm powerless to stop it." Tears cloud my vision, he takes a shuddering breath as he releases me and steps back. "Most of all, I hate that I still fucking love you." I stand here frozen and rooted to the spot as I watch him turn around and head back to the house.

I stand here for so long that my phone ringing is the only thing that snaps me out of my thoughts. Darius loves me, he doesn't hate me! I fish my phone from my bag and curse when I see the time and answer Katie's call.

"Sorry, I'm on my way now!" I say in lieu of a greeting.

"Run bitch run because coach is on a warpath." Shit, I end the call and run as fast I can to get to practice before I get in more shit from coach.

<hr />

I head to my last class of the day, groaning. I fucking hate calculus and Mr. Thompson has it out for me! The asshole has failed me on the last two pop quizzes. I walk into class and head to my usual seat up the back. I drop into my chair and grab out my pad and pen as I wait for Garrett to show up, only he doesn't and Mr. Thompson spends the whole fucking lesson telling us how he doesn't get paid enough to teach idiots. The moment the bell signals the end of class everyone is flying from their desks and racing for the nearest exit trying to escape this fucking room.

I sling my bag over my shoulder as I make my way to the exit. Before I can round the corner to the door, a hand grips my wrist and yanks me into a classroom. I see who it is before I can yell, and stop struggling the moment his lips find mine. He grips my waist and I melt into him, trying to block out the thoughts that taunt me that this won't last, it can't. He groans into my mouth before leaping away from me like I burnt him.

"What happened?" I ask breathlessly.

"If that had lasted another second I would be fucking you against that wall and be late to practice." I bite my lip to stop my smile from breaking free. Darius narrows his eyes playfully. He grips my hand and drags me from the empty classroom after him, then he drops my hand and wraps his arm around my shoulders, drawing me into his side. I don't miss the snide looks and glares that random girls shoot me as we make our way outside. I tense the second we hit the quad and I see my brother and Saint walking toward us. I expect Darius to drop his hold on me but he doesn't and by the looks of things, Corvin views the gesture as a friendly type of thing.

"Well isn't someone looking... flushed." I shoot Saint a warning look that has him laughing and a frown marrying Corv's face.

"You okay?" he asks me.

"Yeah. I'm good but I have to get to practice," I rush to say, I can't be late again or coach will murder me!

"I'll walk you," Darius says. He doesn't wait for a response from my brother as he leads me away from them. I'm a little taken back by his sudden change in attitude and the way he is acting toward me, but I won't question it and risk him going back to not even looking at me in public. He drops me at practice, kisses me on the cheek before running off to his training. Cody and Katie both shoot me wide-eyed looks and I mouth that I will fill them in later.

After practice Katie, Cody and I were too exhausted to go anywhere for food so we grabbed something from the cafeteria before heading to our room to shower and sleep. I'm too exhausted from not sleeping last night to even think about touching my homework. Katie and Cody were out the second their heads hit the pillows, it's not even seven-thirty at night on a Friday and the three of us are in bed. I smile to myself. My phone pings with a message, my heart lurches into my throat thinking it's from that asshole but when I see the name *Big D* flash across my screen I snort out a laugh as I unlock it and read the message.

BIG D

Miss me?

I bite my lip to keep from smiling as I reply.

New fone, who dis?

BIG D

> The guy who had you screaming his name loud enough to wake the dead last weekend.

Now I can't help but laugh at the audacity of him.

> Definitely wrong number, I'm not that type of girl!

BIG D

> Oh but you are the type of girl to drop to your knees in the shower and suck my cock?

Instantly my thighs clench together as I reread his message.

> And are you the type of guy to fuck a girl bare, then push your cum back inside her pussy when it leaks out?

A second passes then my phone begins to vibrate with an incoming call, I bite my lip as I answer it and whisper.

"Hello?"

"You seriously want to send me a fucking message like that and expect me not be rock fucking hard?" The ache between my thighs intensifies knowing that he is rock hard for me.

"You started it," I hiss.

"I didn't think you would reply with that shit!"

"Well, I live to surprise you." He snorts.

"Yeah, you sure fucking do. Where are you?"

"In my dorm?" I don't know why I answered that more like a question.

"Not tonight, get your shit your coming over for the weekend."

"Darius, I can't–"

"I'm out front, you have five minutes before I get someone to let me in and drag your sexy ass out."

"What about Corvin?" There, I addressed the elephant in the room.

"His room is down the hall and he has a party to go to tomorrow so we can fuck in the kitchen while he's gone." I choke on my own spit.

"That's pretty presumptuous," I say before a sigh spills from my lips.

"Spit out whatever is on your mind, Goldie." I take a deep breath and say it.

"Are you gonna kick me out again and hate me when the past creeps up on you?" I hear him exhale and wait with bated breath for his answer. I'm terrified he is going to hang up and end whatever this is between us.

"I'm gonna try. I need you to give me a chance to wrap my head around shit but I also need you to tell me the truth, Leah. After last night I know there is more to the story and when you're... ready to tell me, I'll be here." His words are like a balm to my tattered heart.

"I'll be down in two minutes. Not like I need to pack much since I plan on being naked and under you for the weekend." I end the call before he can reply and smile to myself feeling slightly victorious that I was able to stun him.

CHAPTER TWENTY-FIVE

Darius

I stare at the black screen on my phone for a solid minute, lost for fucking words. This girl is fucking killing me. I'll admit, my actions tonight aren't noble. Corvin is worried as fuck about her and after seeing me with her today, he asked me if I could get her to stay at the house. I lied to her, Corvin isn't going to a party, he's meeting with Troy to sign the last contract and then everything is done, the merger is complete and we can finally move onto phase two of our plan. I of course agreed to help my best friend out. What he doesn't know is she only agreed to stay because my dick is on the menu and I think it best if I leave that part of the story out. The front door of the dorm building opens to reveal Leah, grinning at me with a bag swung over her shoulder. I frown when I take in her fucking outfit.

"What the hell is that?" I growl while pointing to her sports bra and tiny as fuck shorts that leave nothing to the imagination. She rolls her eyes.

"This is what I sleep in. You wouldn't know this because I can't seem to keep clothes on when you're around." I tilt my head side to side not agreeing and not denying her claim either. This is what I love and miss, the banter between us and how easy we can just be ourselves. I need her to open up to me if this is ever going to be more than... what it is.

"Come on, I got Corv's car," I say as I grab her bag from her and lead the way to the parking lot where Corvin's car waits idling. We slip into the car and a light laugh leaves her when she sees Beck in the backseat.

"Why am I not surprised he brought you for backup?" Beck shrugs as he says,

"Had to make sure he didn't need help breaking in to get you out." She laughs, but the truth is what he says isn't far from the truth.

We spend the night hanging out with the guys. It was actually nice to just kick back with them and not think about everything. Leah called it a night about twenty minutes ago and I plan to follow her shortly and spend the night getting lost inside her.

"When are we going to go public with everything?" Saint asks, I turn to him and watch as Crue places a hand on his shoulder offering his silent support. Saint tries to put on a brave face but I know this shit must be fucking hard for him. Out of the five of us, when this thing goes public, it's me and Saint that will wear the brunt of it all.

"We keep it under wraps for a few months before we move onto phase two." Saint nods and tries to hide his feelings behind a mask but he forgets we know him too well and can see the anguish in his eyes. "We'll be here for you every step of the way, brother," Corv tacks on. "I'll finalize everything with Troy tomorrow. Beck will finish out the rest of his schooling online and go to Alaska to learn what he needs to help us." A pang hits me in the chest knowing that Beck is leaving soon. We all have skin in the game but he is the one who has to leave while we stay back.

"Don't look so fucking sad, you pussies!" Beck says on a light chuckle. The rest of us force a smile for his benefit but since high school we haven't been apart, so this is going to be hard. "It's only a couple months and then I'll be back." I stay with the guys for another hour before I call it a night. Beck shoots me a knowing look as I leave them but I know he won't say anything. I make my way upstairs and head for my room. I don't feel tired, when I should after the practice we had today but fuck it, that just means I need to fuck Leah until I pass out. I find her cuddled up in *my* bed.

Smart girl.

I lock the door behind me and for good measure, lock the bathroom door just in case. I strip down to my briefs and climb in beside her. She stirs as I pull her into me and spoon her tiny body. I'm rock fucking hard but I also know she must be tired, so instead of waking her with my face between her legs, I just lay here holding her for hours. When her phone keeps pinging with incoming texts, I debate on leaving it but then it rings. It's two in the fucking morning! I reach over to her side of the bed and grab her phone off the side table and frown at the name.

Piece of shit!

It rings out before I can answer it, and I hold the phone, wondering who the fuck she could hate enough to save their contact info under a name like that. I try to unlock it but of course, there is a fucking passcode! Another message pings through and thank fuck for iPhone's displaying messages on the lock screen.

PIECE OF SHIT

You have until game day to end this!

I stare at the message until the screen turns black again, what the fuck did that mean? What the fuck is she up to and what the hell does our game against the Dolphins have to do with it? I'm too fucking wired to sleep now. I lay here until the sun begins to crest the horizon, only then do I give up on the idea of sleep and slip out from beside her. I grab some clothes and head to the basement, needing to work out my frustrations. I fucking hate not knowing what the hell is going on. I know she is keeping shit hidden and that is fucking with my head! I spend the next hour and a half working out, only stopping when my arms feel like lead. I make my way to the kitchen to make a protein shake before taking it out back.

"You're up early." I look over my shoulder to see Crue walking toward me with a coffee in hand. He runs a hand through his bed hair as he drops down into the lounger beside me. The fucker still wears plaid bed pants to bed and no shirt, even though we told him years ago that they went out of fashion.

"Couldn't sleep," I answer in a flat tone.

"Hm, one would think having a hot blonde next door to you would help you sleep better." He wags his brows at me suggestively. "We all know you want to hit that."

I turn the tables on him, tired of them all knowing my business. "Like we all know you want to *hit* Saint?" He chokes on his coffee, sitting forward, spluttering. I lean over and pat his back fighting my smile. When he finally stops coughing, he pins me with a filthy look.

"What the fuck?" He tries to sound angry but he isn't pulling that shit off.

"You know none of us give a fuck, right?"

He shakes his head. "I don't know—"

"Crue, stop," I cut in. He clamps his mouth closed and lowers his gaze. I swing my legs over the side and rest my hand on the top of his knee. "If you want him, tell him. You know Saint, he lives in the moment and never lets shit get to him so you're gonna need to spell it out for him, brother."

"I'll do it when you tell Corvin about Leah." I sigh knowing that he's right but it isn't the right time.

"My shit is complicated but yours isn't. If it bothers you

seeing him with all these girls then tell him. Don't watch from afar and live your life wondering *what if.*" He nods solemnly.

"I can't tell him." A smile spreads across my face finally hearing him admit it out loud. "He has too much stress on him with this whole business shit and me telling him that I'm in love with him is only going to complicate shit. He needs me and if that means I have to stand by his side and watch him fuck everyone, then so be it because I would rather have him in my life than not at all." I know exactly how he feels and that fucking sucks.

"Just don't wait too long, okay? If he's what you want, then go for it."

"What if... what if he doesn't–"

"Dude, I've seen the way he looks at you. Saint may not know it or even want to acknowledge it but he has feelings for you as well. You're just going to have to give him time to come to terms with the fact that he isn't as straight as he thinks he is." A whoosh of air escapes him.

"You are actually really good at giving advice. You should try taking some of your own." I shove him back and we both laugh.

"I'm the guru, my man. I give advice, not take it."

I spend the day hanging with the guys and Leah in the pool playing volleyball. Her, Crue and Saint against me, Beck and Corv. She gets her shit talking from her brother. The girl can talk so much shit, she has been laying out insults since we started playing. Her and Corvin are so competitive and it's fucking funny to watch them battle it out. I have to admit my attention is constantly pulled to her when she jumps out of the water to hit the ball over the net. Her tits bounce up and down in that yellow bra thing she wears that is tied in so many different fucking knots. Beck spikes the ball over the net and her and Crue dive for it but they crash into each other. The three of us scream and shout that we got a point.

"Shit!" I turn away from Beck and Corv to see her holding the front of her top, my eyes widen when I realize it's come undone. I don't think as I wade through the water to shield her from Crue and Saint's eyes. I duck under the net, grip her waist and push her back until we are in the corner of the pool. I keep my back to the others shielding her, she smiles her thanks as she begins to retie her top. I watch shamelessly biting my bottom lip to suppress the groan that wants to break free, my cock is hard as fuck inside my board shorts.

"The fuck are you doing?" Both our eyes widen at the sound of Corvin's voice, I didn't even think about him as I covered her.

Fuck!

CHAPTER TWENTY-SIX

Leah

My mouth hangs open in shock, Darius's eyes are wide. When I hear the splashing I quickly finish tying my top and not a second too soon, because Darius is yanked away from me to reveal a pissed off looking Corvin standing there. I reach out to grab my brothers arm but he yanks it away as he gets in Darius's face.

"What the fuck was that?" Corvin shouts in his face. Darius schools his features, keeping his face blank and looking bored.

"Would you have rather me let everyone get an eye of her tits?" I flinch at the harsh tone of his voice. Corvin frowns as he looks over to me. I nod agreeing that what Darius says is true.

"My top came undone when Crue and I were diving for the ball, Darius covered me while I fixed it." My voice trembles and I hope like hell he doesn't notice. He turns back to Darius and eyes him warily for a second.

"You better not have looked, dick!" Darius rolls his eyes and shoves Corv playfully. "I mean it, my sister is off limits to all you fuckers." My heart sinks. Darius shoots me a quick glance before swimming back to his side of the pool where

Beck stands waiting. Corvin places his hands on my shoulders and smiles but it doesn't reach his eyes. "Don't get cute with any of these guys because they know touching you would mean the end of the five of us." Unable to speak I just nod and fight to push the feeling of dread out of me.

Corvin left an hour ago to go to some party thing. It's only three in the afternoon so it must not be a good party. The guys and I have been hanging out in the pool all day. I invited Cody and Katie over as well and they have been trying to teach Saint and Crue our routine. Beck and I are laying on the loungers laughing at them while Darius dashed inside to get us some drinks.

"You move like a freaking giraffe!" Cody abolishes as Saint tries to do the *Monestray* dance. "You're so stiff!" She adds, exasperated. Saint stops trying and presses into my friend. Cody doesn't move or even seem affected by his nearness, the reason for that is because I know who she has a crush on.

"I'll show you what's stiff," he says cockily. Cody runs her hand down his naked chest suggestively. Saint smiles triumphantly.

"Oh, baby, if I wanted to prick my vagina with a needle, I'd get a sewing kit." The smile vanishes from Saint's face while the rest of us burst out into fits of laughter.

"What's so funny?" Darius asks as he comes back and hands Beck and I our drinks. I cringe when I see he opted for a protein shake instead of a water.

I'm going straight to hell!

Beck fills him on what happened. Saint shoots us a glare as he pushes Cody in the pool. Not one to be deterred, he moves onto Katie who holds her hand out stopping him before he can get too close.

"I have recently discovered I prefer to eat pussy than suck dick, so unless you're down to have your ass eaten, I'm not the girl for you." Saint throws his head back laughing as he slings his arm around my girl's shoulders and pulls her into his side.

"I think I fucking love you!" Katie rolls her eyes and pushes away from Saint to dive into the pool. I cut a glance to the side to see Crue standing there with a hurt look on his face, my mouth dropping open in shock. I spin to face Darius and Beck. Darius clamps a hand over my mouth and shakes his head.

"Mind ya business, Goldie." My eyes dart between him and Beck, they both knew! "What they get up to behind closed doors does not concern us." I nod and he drops his hand. Feeling like ruffling his feathers, I stand and love the way his eyes travel the length of my body and drink me in.

"Does what we do behind closed doors concern Beckett?" Beck's mouth drops open. Before Darius can reach for me, I take off laughing and jump into the pool laughing so hard I swallow a bit of water before I break the surface.

"So, are you like, living here now?" Cody asks me. Me, Katie and Cody are sitting out on the back deck on the loungers while the guys are inside catching up with Corv. Today has been the best day I have had in months. Hanging out with my brother and the guys, then having the girls come over has made this the best day ever.

"No, I'm just staying here for the weekend," I answer.

"So have you been nailed against the wall yet?" I swat Katie on the arm as the three of us laugh.

Shaking my head, I say, "No, we just slept and it was… nice."

Cody scrunches her face up. "If I was tapping that, the last thing I would be doing is sleeping!" I roll my eyes.

"We all know who you would rather be sleeping with," Katie teases. Cody stiffens, and I place my hand atop hers and smile.

"I would be the world's biggest hypocrite if I told you to stay away from my brother. If you like him then… go for it." Cody stares at me like I have lost my mind. Who knows, maybe I bloody have. We spend the rest of the night laughing and joking around, talking about our dance and if we are really going to do it at the finals. I've never had girlfriends like this before and honestly, it is the most amazing feeling to have friends who don't judge you or want to use you because of who you are related to. Cody and Katie support me and my choices, which is why I would do anything for these girls because friends like this are once in a lifetime type of friends.

Darius and I spend the rest of the night tangled in the sheets. He makes me come so many times that I pass the fuck out, utterly exhausted and spent in the best possible way. When Sunday morning rolls around, the guys decide that we need to pack a picnic and spend the day at the beach. I of course invite my girls who are always down to hang out. I love that they get on with the guys and there is no tension between any of us, just good vibes.

When we sit down to eat, guilt washes over me at the sight of Saint and Darius drinking their pre-made protein shakes they brought from home. I am a shitty fucking person. I spend the rest of the day in a sour mood as the reality of what I'm doing crashes down on me. When it's time to call it a day, I decide to head back with the girls, much to Corvin and Darius's dismay. Truth is, the guilt is eating me alive and won't allow me to be near them any longer.

The girls and I spend the rest of the evening catching up on homework. I ignore the numerous texts and calls from *Big D* and *Piece of shit!* I just need to get through the next few weeks and then everything will be fine. I just hope that they can forgive me when the truth comes out. I just need to finish this and then he will be gone for good and I'll finally be free of this weight on my shoulders.

I manage to avoid Darius and the others for the entire week. With the game coming up they have been training hard and every spare minute they get is spent in the gym, so I've been lucky. When the weekend rolls around, that was more difficult. I had to fake being sick and not wanting to spread my germs to the guys before the big game. Darius blew my phone up nonstop. I've barely been replying to him all week. What the hell do I even say to him, I'm sorry I ruined your life?

He is going to hate me, I can feel it in my heart there is no coming back from what I've done. I'm trying to distance myself from him so when the inevitable happens, I'm hoping the pain won't be as crippling. I'm kidding myself, I know it is going to destroy me but I can't look him in the eyes knowing what I've done.

CHAPTER TWENTY-SEVEN

Darius

She keeps avoiding me!

It's now Wednesday and I am tired of her one or two word replies so I skipped out on training early and wait outside the studio she practices in with her dance team. I check my watch, it's six o'clock so she'll be out any second. The doors open and dancers pile out. I spot her, Cody and Katie laughing as they jog down the stairs. I step out from the shadows right into their path, making them slam to a stop and Leah's eyes widen at the sight of me. We stand here silently for a minute just staring at each other, but then the sound of her nasally voice shatters our moment as she slides up beside me. Leah pulls her gaze from me to glare at Carrie as she clings to my arm.

"Hey handsome, I missed you." I don't take my eyes off Leah, waiting to see what she'll do. Will she finally stake her claim and continue to let her *friend* fawn all over me.

"He didn't miss you," Leah growls. My eyes widen in surprise when she steps forward leaving a sliver of space between us, yanks me free from Courtney's clutches and places my hand on her ass! I stand frozen, waiting to see what she does next. "The next time you think you can touch him,

I'll make sure you don't stick the landing on your next turn out." Her mouth gapes open at Leah's threat.

"Have my sloppy seconds then, bitch." Leah grips the back of my neck and pulls my face down to hers and kisses me. I grip her waist with my other hand and grip her ass tighter. I try to deepen the kiss, horny as fuck but she pulls back and smiles at Callie.

"He was never yours, Chelsea." That's her fucking name! "Just so we are clear, we all know he never fucked you no matter how much you sucked his cock. He just couldn't get hard for you." She better have a fucking good point to this because announcing my performance issue to a crowd is not fucking cool! "Want to know why?" She doesn't give her a chance to answer. "He just used you to try and make me jealous." Chelsea burns red with rage.

"You're nothing. He's slept with half the school and he'll be knocking on my door the second he's over you." Leah chuckles.

"Oh, but babes, you never forget your first love." She doesn't wait for a reply as she grips my hand and leads me away. Katie and Cody stay back laughing and cheering for their friend and the smack down she just laid on the bitch. She doesn't stop walking until we're standing out front of her dorm building. She releases my hand and takes a step back. Confused as fuck at her sudden change in attitude I ask.

"You literally just cocked your leg and pissed on me marking your territory not five minutes ago and now you can't get further away from me. What the fuck is going on, Goldie?" She drops her chin to her chest and scuffs the toe of her shoe along the ground. "Look at me, Leah!" I snap. Her gaze lifts to mine and I see anguish in her green eyes.

"I love you, Darius. I have since I was a kid and I probably will for the rest of my life." I open my mouth to speak but she shakes her head forcing me to wait until she is finished. "I'm so sorry for what I have done, I wish I could take it all back and never transfer here and land you in my shit, but I can't and now you are going to pay the price." Tears streak down her cheeks as I stand here confused as fuck. "Please forgive me because I can't stand the thought of you hating me for the rest of our lives. Just know, I didn't have a choice." Too stunned I stand here and watch as she races inside her building sobbing like her fucking heart just got broken.

What the fuck just happened?

"Darius!" I spin around to see Saint and Beck running toward me with angry looks on their faces.

"What the fuck happened?" I demand when they come to a stop in front of me.

"Dude, we have to go. Coach just called an emergency meeting." Fuck, I follow after them deciding to give Leah some time before I break through that fucking door and demand answers. I'm tired of waiting!

"Bullshit!" I shout.

"I'm sorry, son, you tested positive for narcotics." I stand here brimming with rage and shock, there is no fucking way I could test positive.

"Coach, you know Darius has never touched any of that shit!" Corvin jumps to my defense, Beckett, Saint and Crue all voice their agreement. When the guys said *meeting* I thought they meant with the whole team, instead it's just the five of us, Coach and the two assistant coaches in his office.

"I know, Corvin, which is why I have asked for the urine sample to be re tested but–" I slam my eyes knowing what he is going to say next. "We won't have the results back in time for him to take the field. I'm sorry, son, but you're benched for the game against the Dolphins until we can sort this out." I block out everything else as I stand here spiraling. I've never touched any type of drug, not even weed for the fear of becoming an addict like my mom! I've busted my ass to get ready for this final season, what if I never get to take the field again? Corv leads me from the room. I'm too numb to even think of speaking. I get in the car acting on autopilot.

When Corvin pulls into the driveway, no one makes a move to get out. My mind is reeling with possibilities as to how this could have fucking happened. Yeah, I've had a couple beers but I haven't done any fucking thing else!

"We're down a halfback and tight end," I snap my gaze up to meet Corvin's in the rearview mirror.

"What?" I grit out.

"I tested positive as well." I turn to the side and look at Saint who looks fucking crushed.

"How the fuck did this happen?" I roar. I may not be as good as Saint, Corv and Crue but I fucking love the game. When I had nothing I knew I could always count on football and now that has been ripped away from me.

"I don't know, but we'll figure it out, I swear it." Beckett's words don't bring me any comfort. I get out of the car and slam the fucking door as I storm inside the house. I head straight for my room and that's when I let all the anger out. I start smashing shit and throwing it around my room. Why can't I ever have one thing, one fucking good thing in my life? Corvin comes crashing into my room and wraps his arms around me from behind so I'll stop destroying everything.

"I got you, D. We all got you, brother." I'm breathing so fucking hard I can hear the blood rushing in my ears.

"I didn't fucking do it, Corvin."

"I know you didn't, D. Someone fucked with us and we are going to find out who it is and end them."

"I broke my vow," I whisper. He spins me around to face him and wraps me in a hug.

"You didn't break shit, brother," he says in a pained voice. I vowed the night I moved in with Corv that I would never touch any type of drug, it is the one cardinal rule that I live by. I stand here hugging my best friend trying to think of how this happened, when I start to think about how I haven't been able to sleep, can't sit still for long and have been spending more time than usual in the gym just to try and curb the edge off how I have been feeling.

Holy fuck!

I pull back and stare at Corvin, his eyes widen when he sees the look on my face. "I know who drugged us."

"Who?"

"Your sister." He stumbles back a step, shaking his head.

"Nah, man. Leah would never do that, are you out of your mind?" he yells. I spy the other three standing in the doorway but keep my focus on Corvin. Leah's words to me tonight make sense now, she doesn't want me to hate her because she knew what she had fucking done to me!

"It was her, Corvin," I yell.

"Fuck you, I know your angry but–"

I cut him off. "Pull your head out of your ass, Corvin, you even said yourself she's been acting strange and something is up with her. Leah fucking did this to us."

"Where's your proof?" he snaps.

"I'll get your fucking proof for you and when I do, I never want your sister near this house or near me again. As far as I'm concerned, Leah is dead to me."

CHAPTER TWENTY-EIGHT

Darius

It's game day and I am fucking raging.

Corvin and I have been at odds since Wednesday night. I know I'm fucking right and my point was proven when he tried to call her that night and she sent him to voicemail. He has rose-colored glasses on when it concerns his sister. He needs to realize she is a lying, cheating bitch. How I let myself fall into her orbit again I'll never fucking know!

I skipped yesterday and spent the day fixing my room and didn't bother going today as well. I didn't want to run the risk of bumping into her and strangling the fuck out of her. Sitting on the bench with Saint is fucking killing me, the both of us are itching to be out on that field with our team.

"Fuck, man, we're getting slaughtered!" Saint hisses. I grunt my agreement. Corvin may not think it was Leah but Saint, Crue and I do. She is the only one who had access to our house. The thing that is tearing me up inside is not knowing why the fuck she would do this. What does a dancer gain out of getting two football players benched, but what if it isn't about football and this is just her way of getting payback for me ghosting her?

"I'm gonna kill her," I snarl as the buzzer sounds to signal the end of the third quarter. The defensive and offensive teams huddle around our coach as he tears them a new asshole. Saint and I are banished to the end bench, away from the team so we can't hear shit. The stands are packed with people, there isn't an empty seat in sight. I tear my gaze away from the team as streak of blonde in the stands catches my attention. I grind my teeth so fucking hard when I see it's the bitch who tried to ruin me. She races down the bleachers and runs onto the field.

"What the fuck is she doing?" Saint says as we both climb to our feet. I feel my phone vibrate in my pocket with a text. Saint's phone also pings with and incoming text but we're both too focused on watching her storm toward the Dolphins, or more to the point toward Gary fucking Hayes! My fists clench at my sides as I begin to see red.

"Motherfucker!" I snarl as I stalk across the field. I'm too far away to see what she is saying but she shoves her phone in his face. The fucker laughs and shrugs before saying something back, then out of nowhere, she slaps him across the face.

"Shit!" Saint says in awe, my vision blurs when I see him cock his arm back and punch her in the face. "You're fucking dead, cunt!" Saint screams and he and I break out into a sprint as the crowd goes nuts.

"I'll fucking kill you!" I hear shouts from behind us. Fuck, Corvin saw what just happened. Before we can reach him the huge screen behind where the Dolphins are switches from displaying the score to a… video. Leah is sobbing on the ground, Gary's team mates have gathered around him and are shoving him while a few others crowd around Leah. The video comes into focus and I freeze, my blood runs cold at the sight in front of me. Leah lays naked sprawled out on the bed with a guy whose face you can't see pounding into her. Tears roll down her cheeks, her eyes are open but glazed over, her mouth opens and she whimpers out a name.

My fucking name!

The tone of her voice in that video, it's filled with fear and confusion and that is what has me snapping out of it and charging after Gary. I know it's him in that video, I recognize the fucking room as the one I walked in on and found her in that fucking bed! Corvin blitzes past me and tackles Gary to the ground. His arms start swinging as he lands punch after punch. Gary's team mates pull him off their captain but I'm on him next, landing right hook after right hook to his fucking face. I shrug off the fuckers who try to pull me off him. This isn't how I wanted to take the fucker down but it feels fucking marvelous to finally get my pound of flesh.

"You're gonna kill him," someone shouts, the moans coming from the videos around the field fueling my need for his blood. An arm wraps around my throat and waist and yanks me off the bastard. He's groaning on the ground like the fucking piece of shit he is... *Piece of shit.*

I still in Beckett's hold as I turn my head to see Crue holding Leah as she sobs into his chest. It all clicks into place as I dart my gaze between her and Gary. He's the one who was blowing up her phone, he told her she had until game day, she did this for him. I break free of Beckett's hold and march over to her. Crue shoots me a warning look but I ignore it as I look at Leah. Her cheek is red and already starting to bruise, her eyes plead with me to understand.

"You drugged *me* for him?" I shout as she flinches at the harsh tone of my voice. "Why the fuck did you do it?" I yell.

"I... I didn't have a choice!" she cries, assuming she did it is one thing but hearing her admit it out loud cuts me so fucking deep. "He said if I didn't, he would post that video everywhere." Said video is playing on repeat in the background, it's then I realize that the message Saint and I got earlier is probably from an unknown number with a link to the video of him fucking her.

"You could have come to me!" I roar.

"And tell you what, Darius?" she screams. I feel Beckett and Corvin behind me but I keep my focus on her.

"The fucking truth, Leah! You could have told me the fucking truth." She throws her hands in the air.

"Fine. You want the truth here it is. Gary Hayes spiked my drink at that party and raped me to get one up on you." The air whooshes from my lungs. "I found out when I overheard him bragging to his friends at DCU. When I confronted him, he showed me the video and threatened to post it unless I took the five of you out. I didn't even know it had happened until I saw the video!" Crue steps away from her as Corvin comes to my side.

"Why the fuck didn't you say anything?" Corvin shouts. I ignore him as I address her, letting her see all the anger in my eyes.

"You could have come to me the moment you found out, I fucking told you I loved you!"

"You what?" Corvin snaps but I push on.

"I would have fucking ended the son of bitch before this ever got out." I wave my hand around the stadium gesturing to the screens displaying the video. "But no, you wormed your fucking way back into my life like the snake I always knew you were and fucked me over so good. You broke my cardinal vow and I didn't even have a fucking say in the matter!" I scream in her face. "You are done, Leah, there will never be an us again. You know better than anyone what drugs mean to me and still you fucking played me. Well done, baby, that was the one play I didn't see coming."

"You've been fucking my sister?" Corvin pushes in front of me, blocking his sister from my view. I take a shuddering breath as I brace for this shit show to blow up in front of everyone, except I don't get a chance to answer.

"Your sister is a fucking slut and has been fucking your best friend for years!" I whirl around to Gary using the bench seat to try to push himself to his feet. I don't think, I just act. I close the space between us, and hold his hand on the bench with my own as I apply all my weight to stomp down on his elbow relishing in the scream that tears from him when his bones break.

"You'll never throw another fucking ball again, your career is over, you cunt." I'm rushed from all sides, coaches and players step in to break up the fight. Shouts are heard from all around but I can't keep the smile off my face knowing I just ended the fuckers dream of making it big in the NFL.

"You're done!" The sound of his voice has the hairs on the back of my neck rising, I turn my head to the side to see Victor Hayes standing right there. The bastard looks murderous, he stands there in his thousand-dollar suit, brown hair slicked back to try look young but his brown eyes betray him and show his age. I feel Saint and Crue stiffen on either side of me as they let go of my arms, they know what this means for me. "You are going to fucking pay for that, you have no idea what the fuck you have just done!"

Thank You!

Well shit, do ya hate me a wee bit?
I know I suck but cliffhangers are a must and book 2 will be
out next month!
God, I hope you loved these two because I am head over
heels for them, how about that scene with Beck though? Got
to admit that one nearly didn't make it in here but I thought it
was fitting to chuck Mr tall dark and broody in the mix for
you, you're welcome.

You may have thought Darius was an asshole in this book,
just wait till you see what he does in book 2.

Seriously though, thank you so freaking much for reading
Offside. I always knew I wanted to write a bully duet and just
now had the gumption to do it. I am so in love with this
world and these characters, I never want to leave it!

I hope you are ready for *Touchdown* because holy shit balls I
am! Just wait till you see the damage and chaos that ensues in
the next one, I swear the wait is worth it.

THANK YOU!

From the bottom of my heart, thank you for ready Darius and Leah's book it means more than you will ever know xxx

If you loved Offside, please leave a review on Amazon, Bookbub or Goodreads.
Reviews are like tips for us authors, the more reviews we get the more exposure the book gets.

Also by Samantha Barrett

PARANORMAL ROMANCE

The Dream Series

The Dream Trilogy

A Beautiful Dream

A Twisted Fate

A Beautiful Nightmare

Redemption

Anarchy

Brutal Savages

Savage Lies

Brutal Truth

Savage Beast

Brutal Beauty

MAFIA ROMANCE

Murdoch Mafia Series

Played By The Bishop

Tormented By The King

Tortured By The Knight

Tempted By The Queen

Turned By The Pawn

Ruined By The Rook

Acknowledgments

Leah, my girl this duet wouldn't be here without you and your crazy story! Thank you for trusting me and allowing me to tell your story with a few twists and making it dark. Thank you for the amazing cover for these books and all the graphics, ILY.

Marcus, baby daddy, my nightly D ride. Thanks for helping me plot out the sex scenes in this book and still not sorry you have blue balls.

Tash, thank you, thank you, thank you. I don't know what else I can say aside from that. No words can describe how grateful I am for you, thank you for letting me use your maiden name for Leah. Xxx

Clare Bear, Sarah, my beta girls, thank you both so much for loving Darius and helping me rewrite the ending until it was perfect. You, ladies, are amazing and I adore you more than you know.

My main team, there is too damn many of you to name lol I love you so freaking much, you ladies always keep me humble and make sure my ass writes these books on time. I love you all so much and thank you for being a part of my team it means the world to me.

Lizz, my amazing as fuck editor, you are the best and I cannot thank you enough for all the work you put into these books and for always slotting me in when I need it. Thank you xxx

My babies, you both inspire the asshole side of Darius with how often you fight and constantly make me want to tear my hair out. I love you both but for the love of God please stop fighting like a pack of girls on PMS week.

Last but not least, my amazing readers,
Thank you from the bottom of my cold dead-ass heart for loving all these books and taking a chance on me. Your support and love is the reason why I get to live out my dream of being an author, I appreciate each and every one of you.
I love you.

Sam
Xxxx

About the Author

Samantha Barrett is a dark romance, PNR author who loves to write out-of-the-box stories. She is originally from the land of the long white cloud, New Zealand. She is totally fluking her way through this whole author gig, if she isn't writing you can find her kicking back with her kids and husband with a bag of chips and a glass of wine in her hand.
Sam loves Twilight and is a TWIHARD proudly.